THE WEDDING HOAX

A MIRACLE BABY ROMANCE

FAUX LOVE BILLIONAIRES

CRYSTAL MONROE

Copyright © 2023 by Crystal Monroe

All rights reserved.

No part of this book may be reproduced in any form or by any electronic or mechanical means, including information storage and retrieval systems, without written permission from the author, except for the use of brief quotations in a book review.

BONUS NOVELLA

Get a spicy secret baby romance delivered to your inbox.

Grab your copy of Second Chance Daddy here!

https://BookHip.com/CDDJPXR

1

SIMONE

"Did you want your coffee black?" A bored barista was staring back at me, like she desperately wanted to roll her eyes.

"Could I get a splash of almond milk? Or maybe oat milk." I laughed nervously.

I was starting a new job as a staff writer at *LA Now*. I'd decided to check out the trendy coffee shop across the street from the building.

Which may have been a total mistake, judging by the barista's new, annoyed expression. "So, which is it? Almond or oat?"

I smiled. "You know what? I'll go with the—"

"Can I get the usual, Sandy?" A deep voice was suddenly booming next to me, a sense of command in the stranger's every word.

I looked over and saw a sharp vision in an even sharper suit. He was tall, with an angular jaw and intense eyes. His dark brown hair was slightly tousled on top in that perfect way guys like him always pulled off.

There was also the matter of just how well he was filling

out his suit, his muscles leaving an imprint against the fabric—

Wait.

Did this asshole just cut in front of me?

"Hey!" I chimed into the conversation.

"Oh. Hey." The stranger seemed almost as annoyed as the barista. "Did you need something?"

"Yeah. I need you to get behind me."

It took everything in me not to let my cheeks flush at the thought of the stranger actually *getting behind me.*

"How about I pay for your drink instead?" he suggested with a shrug. "I've got places to be this morning, so I'd rather Sandy take care of me first if it's all the same to you."

"It's not all the same to me." I stood my ground. "The rules apply to everybody, buddy. If we all just start cutting in line because we're busy, society will break down within months."

"Really? Months?" He let out a tired sigh. "I was hoping it'd be weeks. Maybe even days."

And then a small grin crept across his face.

"Jerk." It was my turn to roll my eyes.

I looked back at Sandy across the counter. "Sandy, could you get that coffee going for me, please? I'll go with the oat milk."

"Got it. Coming right up." Sandy nodded as I tapped my card against the reader. "And don't call me Sandy. Only the people I like get to call me that."

"You're going to like me, Sandy! One day! I promise!" I called out after her as she went toward the back of the coffee shop. "I'm very likable!"

"Clearly." Mr. Big Shot laughed as he settled in line behind me.

It was the last thing he said to me before Sandy handed

us our coffees at the same time. Her face was blank as she gave me my cup, even though she beamed when she handed Mr. Big his to-go coffee.

Of course, he was drowning in female attention.

Even though he was probably too *busy* to notice.

"Thank you," I said to Sandy as I took my cup. With slumped shoulders, I carried it to a booth at the back of the coffee shop, tucked away in the corner.

I stared in my cup for a long moment, trying to calm my nerves.

LA Now was one of the top magazines in Los Angeles, and this staff writer position could really change things for me.

There was a lot riding on my new job.

I hoped I wouldn't botch it like I did ordering coffee.

"Simone!"

The voice of my best friend made me look up, snapping me back to reality. Taylor grinned as she walked over to the booth, carrying her latte.

"Taylor! I didn't see you come in," I said.

Taylor was my best friend and the reason I'd been able to get a job at *LA Now* in the first place, since she was one of the best editors on their staff. She was also one of the best people I'd ever met, period, which is why I was already grinning like a maniac at the sight of her.

"Are you ready for your first day?" She took a seat across from me.

"Yes, I'm ready! Kind of. Well, maybe not." I nervously chuckled again. "What happens if I get fired on my first day? As in, how bad would that look on my resume?"

She laughed. "You're not going to get fired on your first day."

"You said the CEO can be moody." I fidgeted with my napkin.

"Harry might be a bit of an asshole, but he's not a *total* asshole. He only fires people on day one if they piss him off beyond belief."

"What pisses him off beyond belief?"

"Nothing you'd ever do." She thoughtfully took a sip of her latte. "You're too nice of a person to piss anyone off."

"I pissed off Sandy."

"Sandy? The barista?" Taylor's mouth fell open. "Really? But she's so sweet to everyone! What'd you do?"

"Nothing! I just took a little too long to get my coffee order together. Then this guy came in, cut the line and tried to order ahead of me, and I let him know I wasn't having it. I might have called him a jerk."

"Shit." Taylor's eyes went wide.

"Shit?"

"Was he wearing a really nice suit? Handsome in a suspicious way? Like, almost impossibly handsome?"

"Yeah? How'd you know?"

"That's Harry. Our boss." She grimaced. "He has a habit of thinking the world revolves around him. Probably because it does. Anyway, he cut me in line when I first got here, too."

"And? What'd you do?"

"I let him do it because I knew he was the boss."

"Right. That's smart. Much smarter than calling him a jerk."

"You'll be fine. Don't let it get to you." Taylor shook her head. "When you see him in the office, just pretend it never happened, like you two never met before."

"Lying to my boss feels worse than not letting him cut in line—"

"And being unemployed feels worse than anything else," she interrupted. "Just promise me you'll do what I say. Okay?"

"I promise I'll think about it."

"Close enough."

∼

Two hours later, Taylor and I stood in the copy room in the offices of *LA Now*.

"Do you want me to show you how to work the copier again?" Taylor asked, playfully patting its side. "Don't be ashamed if it takes you a few tries to get it. It practically took me a month."

"How are you so bad with technology? Doesn't your family own a computer shop?"

"Rude. You're being so rude right now." Taylor scoffed playfully. "Seriously, though. Do you need anything else? This is the last thing to cover on your orientation."

I thought about the question for a minute. She'd been assigned to show me around the office and introduce me to the other writers and editors on staff.

Unfortunately, she'd also been responsible for helping me set up my laptop and email. She was clearly out of her league there, and I'd told her I could handle it on my own.

Or maybe I'd just leave a desperate SOS message on an IT guy's voicemail.

"I think I've got it." I smiled back at her. "But..."

"But?"

"But maybe you could show me to Harry's office? So I can apologize before he comes out here and fires me—"

"If you interrupt Harry while he's in a meeting, he'll *defi-*

nitely fire you." Taylor leaned against the copier. "Like I said, just pretend it never happened."

"Right."

I couldn't admit to Taylor the real reason why I wanted to be introduced to Harry.

A part of me just wanted to *see* him, to make sure my eyes hadn't been lying to me the first time.

Sure, he was an asshole, and sure, he was my boss, but that man was a work of art.

Or maybe I was just a little thirsty for male attention, especially since I hadn't been with anyone since my disaster of an ex—

"Are you still standing here?" Taylor interrupted my thoughts, her tone lined with disbelief. "Go! Get to work!"

"Sir, yes, sir." I saluted with a grin before I headed to my office.

I tried to push all thoughts of Harry away. But his perfect, annoying face keep popping up in my mind.

Working for him wasn't going to be easy.

2

HARRY

No one talked to me like that.

The woman at the coffee shop had completely thrown me off in the very best way, my whole morning gone out the window. I couldn't get her out of my head.

Not her deep hazel eyes, and not her auburn hair that cascaded down her shoulders.

Fuck.

I wanted to talk to her again. I wanted to brush my fingers across her cheek, run my hands through her hair, push her up against the counter and—

"Sir? Your father's here to see you." Paul, my executive assistant, was suddenly standing in front of my desk. "Do you want me to tell him you're busy?"

"No. Send him in." If I sent Dad away, he'd just pester me until I talked to him. And I knew exactly what he wanted to talk about.

Paul nodded before leaving my office. A few seconds later, my dad stepped through the door. He was wearing a Hawaiian shirt, despite his usual gruff exterior. Retirement seemed to have that effect on people, softening them out over time. Even if it was just their clothing choices.

"Son."

"Dad."

"I just wanted to check up on you," he started. "You're always so busy nowadays. I figured finding you at the office would be a safe bet."

"That's what you want, isn't it? The kind of son who works hard. The kind of son who wants to take over the company someday—"

"The kind of son who's going to be married soon, I hope?" He interrupted. "You know the rules, Harry. If you're not married by your fortieth birthday, I won't be able to officially hand you the keys to the company."

"You hear how that sounds, right? Married by my fortieth birthday? It's like a fucked-up fairy tale."

"Language."

"Sorry. It's like a fucked-up fucking fairy tale—"

"That's always how it's been in our family, Harry. You've known that your whole life. We were never going to break tradition just because you don't respect it."

"So, what? All of my years running this place don't count for anything?"

"I'm proud of you for stepping up, Harry. More proud than I've ever been... but no. That doesn't change the tradition."

"If I'm not running the company, then your only other option is Sean." I scoffed. "I love my little brother, sure, but he doesn't have any experience in publishing, Dad. I don't even know if he likes it."

"He works for a magazine, same as you—"

"He works in the IT department! And he works at *Front*

Stoop—our competition!" I scoffed again. "Dad, come on. You can't be serious with this."

"You're the one who needs to get serious, Harry," he replied. "When are you going to settle down? Find someone to build with? To share your life with?"

"I already have someone like that in my life. Her name is *LA Now*."

"Funny." My dad wasn't smiling as he spoke. "Is that really all you want your legacy to be? Is that the kind of legacy you think our family name deserves?"

"Maybe I'm not the marrying type."

"If you're not the marrying type, then you're not fit to be CEO. You don't know how to commit to something bigger than financial spreadsheets and quarterly reports? Then you don't know how to commit to anything—"

"It's under control," I blurted out, cutting my father off.

"What?"

"It's under control," I repeated. "Just because I'm not the marrying type doesn't mean that I haven't met someone. I never said I was single."

"Are you serious?" My dad's face brightened. "You met someone?"

"Yes, and she's like you. Extremely ready for me to settle down, even if I think we need more time, even if I don't want to be forced into it because of *tradition*—"

"She sounds like a smart girl." He beamed. "When do your mother and I get to meet her?"

I huffed. "I need to get back to work. We can discuss all this later when I don't have back-to-back meetings."

"Sure, sure. Of course." He seemed relieved as he stood up. "We'll talk about it later, son. Good job. As always."

"Thanks, Dad."

I watched him walk out the door and swallowed.

What had I just done?

Was I really going to fake my own wedding just to keep the company?

It didn't have to be real. All I had to do was hire an actress or a model to pretend to be my fiancée, maybe hire some paparazzi to follow us around, maybe even have them meet my mom and dad—

No.

All of that felt so wrong. And yet, I was running out of options. I was turning forty in two months, and unless I came up with a better idea, all of my work at *LA Now* was about to go right down the drain.

I couldn't believe my parents would let my brother take over as CEO. I loved Sean, I really did, but he had no clue what he was doing when it came to running a magazine.

Computers were his scene, not running a magazine or managing people.

Which meant that if I wanted to keep the company, I had no choice but to get married.

Shit.

"It's happy hour! Shouldn't you look, I don't know, happy?" Paul asked as he slid a shot glass toward me.

We were catching up after work over drinks, a ritual between us ever since I'd hired him as my assistant. Outside of work, Paul was the opposite of formal, with a laid-back vibe and perfectly messy hair. He also dropped the *sirs*, which was great since otherwise our whole friendship would've been super uncomfortable.

"I am happy, Paul. See? Don't I look happy?" I forced a smile. "I've never been happier."

"Liar." He laughed. "Seriously, man. What's up?"

"Nothing." I lied with a shrug. I didn't see the point in telling him the truth behind my father's visit. It wasn't going to change anything. "Just a rough day at work."

"As usual." Paul laughed again. "When are you going to start getting used to these rough days? Because I'm pretty sure those are the only kind of days that CEOs get to have."

"No, I'm pretty sure they get straight-up bad days, too. And vacation days, in their dreams."

"They also get the fun option of working through major holidays. I mean, who doesn't want to clock in on Christmas Day?"

"Sometimes, Paul, I feel like you're trying to talk me out of my job."

"Ha! No way. You think I want to be some other guy's assistant?" He quickly downed the shot in front of him. "I'm just messing with you, man. Sorry you had a rough day."

"Thanks."

"Drinking might help," he said as he nodded down toward my still untouched shot glass.

"I don't think drinking like a frat boy is going to help anything," I joked, motioning for the bartender to take my drink. "I'll have a whiskey, please. Neat."

"Can you make that two, actually? Both on that guy, right over there." Taylor pointed toward Paul as she spoke before she appeared between us at the bar.

"Taylor!" Paul happily wrapped his arms around her, then pulled her into a big hug. "Thanks for coming out!"

"Please. You know I'll always come out for you, Paul." She beamed. "Although, I hope you don't mind. I invited a friend out with us tonight."

"Is she going to kill the vibe?"

"Not on purpose, no." A familiar voice answered the question with a laugh. "But if I somehow kill the vibe tonight, I accept full responsibility. All apologies in advance."

Holy shit.

It was her.

The woman from the coffee shop was standing right next to me.

When our eyes locked, she suddenly looked away like she was nervous. I was taken aback by her response.

After our run-in this morning, she didn't seem like the kind of person who'd ever back down first.

"Sorry," she started. "I didn't know you were going to—Taylor didn't tell me—"

"That we were having drinks with the boss? Absolutely not," Taylor replied. "If I did, you never would've agreed to come out with us."

"The boss?" My eyes went wide. "Wait. *You* work for *me*?"

"Yep. Simone Didier. New staff writer at *LA Now*. Pleasure to meet you." She awkwardly held out her hand.

And I completely ignored the gesture. "Why are you acting like this is our first time meeting each other?"

"Oh. Have we met before?"

"You weren't the crazy lady talking about the fall of society in the coffee shop this morning?"

"Doesn't sound like me." Her face was stone.

I couldn't help but laugh. "You really are something else, aren't you?"

"Something like that, yeah." She nodded along with her words. "Anyway, I'm actually feeling really tired. Long first day, you know? I think I might head out—"

"Nope. Can't leave yet," Taylor interrupted. "Paul and I

need to go say hi to a few of our other friends, and then we'll circle back."

"Gotta make the rounds," Paul added, falling in line behind Taylor as they headed away from the bar. "Especially if we're trying to firm up our team for bar trivia next weekend."

"You work the girls, I'll work the boys?" Taylor asked.

"Sounds like a plan," Paul said.

I watched as they both walked away, leaving me alone with her.

Simone.

I glanced at her out of the corner of my eye as she fidgeted with a napkin.

The awkward silence stretched out between us. I craned my neck to see Taylor and Paul working the room, toasting and living it up with various people in every corner of the bar. It was pretty impressive, even if it was also pretty annoying, watching them work their extrovert magic.

"I'm not sorry."

"What was that? I could barely hear you."

"I'm not sorry," Simone repeated, jutting her chin out. "About what happened at the coffee shop."

"Oh? So, now you remember meeting me back at the coffee shop?"

"It was Taylor's idea to pretend like it never happened," she confessed. "She was worried you were going to fire me."

"I don't fire people over such small slights."

"It wasn't a slight, though, was it? You were trying to cut in front of me. I was there first."

"Sure, but I offered to buy your drink. I had a morning meeting to get to—"

"You're not more important than other people."

"Are you always this self-righteous, Simone? Will your

head explode if I tell you that life has a shit ton of gray areas?"

"Are you always this obnoxious? Why can't you just say sorry for doing something wrong?"

"How about we both apologize on the count of three?" I suggested.

"Not going to happen." She scoffed. "Only one of us owes the other an apology, and it's not me."

There she went again, talking to me in a way no one did.

It was such a turn-on.

In that moment, I wanted to kiss her, to crush my lips against hers, just to see if she'd push me away or kiss me back.

I couldn't deny that I was attracted to everything about her—her defiance, the way she stood her ground, even her self-righteousness, too.

There was something so raw about her. I wasn't used to people being that way around me, especially not as a CEO. People were either kissing my ass or trembling in fear.

But not Simone. Simone was refreshing, like a glass of ice water on a hot summer day.

"Can I buy you a drink?" I asked, my eyes raking up and down her delicious frame, spending a little too long on her chest.

"If that's your way of saying you're sorry, sure," she shot back.

I smirked as I once again called for the bartender's attention.

I wasn't sure what it was about this woman, but she drove me crazy.

In a very, very good way.

3

SIMONE

"Tell me about your family."

"What?" I'd been sipping on a whiskey sour, half-distracted. I was keeping an eye on Taylor as she moved throughout the room, hoping that she'd *circle back* to the bar any second now and rescue me from this awkward situation.

I was having drinks with my boss.

Seriously?

I was dying on the inside. It didn't help that I'd decided to idiotically stick up for myself, either.

"Tell me about your family," he calmly repeated. "How's the drink, by the way?"

"Great. Really great, actually. And as for my family…"

"I get it. You don't want to go first." He chuckled. "Keeping your cards close to your chest."

He took a deep breath before he went on. "My family is ruining my life."

"Really?"

"Really. They're so obsessed with following tradition they can't see the forest for the trees." He pinched the bridge of his nose, frustration rolling off him. "I love them. I do. But they're so close to turning everything into shit and they don't even realize it."

"Sorry. I'm confused."

"Confused?"

"Didn't your family start this magazine years ago and basically give you your job?" I replied. "I mean, aren't they super influential or something?"

"Yes and yes."

"That's why I'm confused, then. That seems like the kind of thing to be thankful for," I said. "I'm sure a lot of people would love to have a leg up like that. It makes everything so much easier."

"Easy to say when you're standing outside of it all."

Easy to say when you were born rich, prick.

I briefly thought about my own family, my dad's funeral flashing through my mind. I took another sip of my drink, pushing away the memory.

"Your turn." He smirked. "What's your family like?"

"They're fine."

"Really? That's all? After I just spilled my guts?"

"It's just me and my mom." I shrugged. "There's not much to say."

"Fine, then. Change of topic. What's the craziest thing you've ever done?"

"Uh, pulled an all-nighter back in college. Ordered like twenty pizzas to the dorms. Caused complete chaos. Oh, and sometimes I'd sneak some vodka in a water bottle before going to class."

"Are you serious?" Harry slowly blinked. "Please tell me you're joking."

"What's wrong? Not crazy enough for you?"

He leaned toward me with a wicked grin. "I'm just

surprised. A woman who looks like you... I just figured you'd be getting into all kinds of trouble."

His eyes stayed on me as he spoke, heat momentarily flashing in his gaze. My face started to burn in response, as I felt my cheeks flush a deep red. He was so close to me now that all he had to do was lean over a few more inches for our lips to touch, for us to be skin to skin.

God, I wanted him to lean over a few more inches.

It didn't help that he smelled like heaven—woodsy, clean, and expensive. The kind of man who went skiing in his free time and stayed in the most luxurious cabins.

Just then, he shifted back into place, moving away from me. "I think I'm starting to figure you out, Simone."

"Figure me out?"

"Yep. You're a Goody Two-Shoes." He chuckled. "That's why you're so self-righteous, right? You spend so much time following the rules, you think everyone else should, too."

"Are we still on this?" I chuckled, too, in disbelief. "I thought you apologized when you bought me a drink!"

"I never agreed to those terms."

"You're right. I should've read the fine print."

"You've always got to read the fine print, Simone. Always." He flashed a smile before downing the rest of his whiskey.

And I couldn't help the way my eyes lingered on his lips, wondering how they'd taste if I closed the gap between us at the bar.

~

"Mom! Did you want red sauce or white?"

Two hours later, I was in the kitchen at home, prepping a quick dinner of pasta. Taylor had taken mercy on me after an hour or so at the bar and thankfully dropped me off at the apartment I shared with my mother.

"I think red sauce sounds good for tonight," my mom replied, her motorized wheelchair buzzing its way into the kitchen, too. "But what are you in the mood for?"

"Whatever you're in the mood for, Mom."

"You know you don't have to do that." She sighed. "Cater to me like this because of… the accident. I'm still your mom. I'm supposed to be taking care of you, not the other way around."

Because of the accident.

I winced away from the memory, even though it played as clear as day in my head.

Nine years ago, my parents had been in a horrific car wreck. My dad had been instantly killed by the impact, while my mom fought for her life at the hospital. A few weeks later, she was released, but she wasn't the same.

The accident had not only taken her husband, it'd taken the use of her legs, too. She'd been paralyzed from the waist down ever since, even though she pretended like nothing much had changed. She was keeping a brave face for me, despite all the pain.

And I tried to do the same. "I'm not catering to you because of the accident, Mom. I'm just not particular about my pasta sauces."

"Liar." She chuckled as she handed me a black pepper shaker. "Smells like it could use more seasoning."

"Hey! Back off, lady," I joked. "Two chefs is too many chefs in the kitchen."

"Uh-huh. Right." My mother squinted, like she was trying to get a better view of the pan. "How was your first day of work at your new job, Simi?"

"Good. Until Taylor bamboozled me into having drinks

with the boss."

"Oh? Is your boss nice?"

"Nice?" I took the salt my mom was handing to me as I spoke. "I wouldn't say he's nice. He's maybe Jerk Lite? Still, he did buy me a drink. But he won't apologize for trying to cut in front of me for coffee this morning. And he doesn't seem to appreciate how lucky he is when it comes to being born rich, which is annoying for an entirely different reason—"

"Uh-oh."

"What? Did I put too much salt in the pan?" I panicked, moving my hand away from the stove.

"You're talking about him a lot. When all I asked was a simple question." My mom shook her head. "You know what that means, don't you?"

"That I'm giving him way too much of my headspace when I should be focused on making dinner?"

"That you like him."

"Absolutely not!" I shot back. "Mom, he's not my type. At all. He's basically a trust fund rich kid who lucked into running a company. And even if he was my type, Taylor says he's obsessed with *LA Now,* which means he wouldn't have time for a relationship, anyway—"

"Wow, you've really thought this through," my mom muttered.

"Go! Out of the kitchen!" Flustered, I motioned for her to leave. "I'll bring you dinner when it's all done!"

"It's okay for you to have fun sometimes, Simone." She smiled. "Things don't always have to be so serious."

I smiled back at her. "I know, Mom. Seriously, though. I need to finish up this pasta so we can actually eat something tonight."

"Or we can just order out..."

"Mom!" I pretended to be wildly upset, as I threw my hands up in the air. "Are you suggesting that I'm not the best cook in all of Los Angeles?!"

"You know what? You're right. I believe in you, Simi." My mom chuckled as she turned her wheelchair around, heading out of the kitchen. "Besides, all the good restaurants are closed by now, anyway."

4

HARRY

I'd been thinking about her all night.

I couldn't have stopped even if I tried. She was stuck in my head like a way-too-catchy song, despite my best efforts to get her out of my mind.

There was just something about how honest she was with me, how she was never afraid to tell me exactly what she was thinking.

And I couldn't lie, the fact that she never backed down was sexy as hell.

Shit. Was this the most honest connection I'd had with a woman in months? Years?

I knew that Simone wasn't after me for my money, at least, which was a pretty good start. Hell, she'd probably slap me in my face if I even suggested taking her out for dinner. It wouldn't be appropriate for a Goody Two-Shoes like her to go out with her boss, after all.

But what if I wasn't her boss? What if I was something more?

"Mr. O'Donnell?" Simone popped her head in my open door and interrupted my train of thought.

I gestured for her to sit down, and she took a seat across the desk from me. She was wearing a pencil skirt that hugged her round hips. Her sleeveless blouse skimmed over her perky tits. It was her second day of work, and she was already driving me crazy with that killer figure.

When I didn't say anything, lost in thought, she tilted her head.

"You called me into your office?" she asked. "You wanted something, I assume?"

"Right." I coughed to buy myself more time. What I was about to suggest was *insane*. I needed to be sure I pitched it perfectly. "It was fun hanging out at the bar last night, wasn't it?"

"Something like that. Sure."

"Do you think you could do more of that? For a few months, maybe?"

"Do what?"

"Hang out with me."

"Oh, God." She groaned. "Did Taylor sign us up for the same bar trivia team or something? I told her I'm not good under that kind of pressure—"

"Would you..." I cleared my throat. "...marry me?"

"I'm sorry? I think I misheard you." Simone slowly blinked. "Did you just ask me to—"

"Remember how I told you my family is so obsessed with tradition that they can't see the forest for the trees?" I shrugged. "This is what I was talking about. They want me married by my fortieth birthday or else I'm out as CEO."

"Wait. What?" Simone shook her head. "But you're good at this. That profile of you in *Forbes* said that you saved this place from bankruptcy a million times over."

"You read that profile of me in *Forbes*?" I smirked. "Ms. Didier, have you been cyberstalking me?"

The Wedding Hoax

"Don't let it go to your head. I was just doing research about my boss. It's not that weird."

"Whatever you say." I smirked even wider. "Still. If I don't get married soon, I'm out of the company. If I don't at least feign interest in carrying on the family line, they'll replace me with my brother." I winced. "Sean works in IT. He doesn't know how to run *LA Now* unless we're talking about running it into the ground."

"So, what? You want me to marry you just so you can keep your job?" She scoffed.

"It wouldn't be permanent. I think six months should suffice. If you agree, I'd have us sign a contract. And I'd pay you for your time, of course. I was thinking something around half a million?"

"I have to go, actually. There's somewhere else I suddenly need to be." She abruptly stood up and turned away from me. "Thanks, but no thanks, Mr. O'Donnell."

"Wait! Just give me a chance to explain!"

But it was already too late. Simone was headed down the hall, her feet moving so fast it almost seemed like she was running for her life.

~

Hours passed, with no Simone in sight.

I briefly wondered if I'd somehow ruined my professional career, just by asking her a question. Was she gossiping about me to the rest of the staff writers? Was she on the phone with a lawyer, wondering if she could build a lawsuit against me?

I shuddered at the thought.

"How would the money work?"

Simone's voice was low as it floated across my office. It

was nearly 5:00 p.m. and she now stood in the doorway, like she was hesitating to come inside.

"I mean, if I said yes?" she asked.

"Close the door and I'll tell you everything you want to know."

She nodded, then closed the door behind her. "Would you pay it out in pieces? Or would I get the whole thing upfront?"

Damn. Maybe she'd been after my money, after all.

"It's just my mom," she continued. "She was in a pretty bad car accident a few years ago. She hasn't been able to walk since then. Anyway, there's this experimental surgery that could give her some mobility back and maybe help with the pain, too. But since it's experimental, insurance won't cover it."

I was flooded with relief at her admission. "We can work it out, however you need. Just let me know how much it'll cost and I'll wire the money to you as soon as everything's settled."

"Okay." She nodded again. "Okay, then. I think I can do it."

"You think you can do it? Really?"

"I mean, I'm not much of an actress. But you said it'd only be for a few months, right?"

"Right."

"Then, yeah. I think I can pretend to be your wife for a few months." She folded her arms in front of her chest. "What's that going to be like, anyway? Like, do I actually have to meet your family?"

"Yes. You'll have to live with me, too."

"Separate rooms?" she pressed.

"Of course," I assured her. "We won't be doing anything

you're not comfortable with. Although, you won't be able to see anyone else while we're doing this, so if there's someone you had your eye on—"

"You don't need to worry about that." She held up a hand. "Besides, I imagine my dating someone else would look pretty bad to your family. Like you got married but you have a bad picker."

"Or like my marriage isn't real, which would be even worse. That would definitely be grounds for handing things over to Sean."

"No sex."

"What was that?"

"There won't be any sex," she demanded. "I understand needing to be lovey-dovey around your family and hold hands. But I don't have to be intimate with you. Ever."

"Sure, but is that something you really want me to put in the contract?" I playfully winked. "You spend enough time with someone, who knows what could happen?"

"I won't sign it if it's not in there." Her tone was serious. "No sex. And then I'll sign on the dotted line."

"Got it. No sex." I sat back in my office chair. "I'll draw the contract up myself. It'll be in your inbox in a few hours."

"Sounds great. I think I'm going to head out now."

"Yeah, you should. I like the business casual look, but I think you might want to wear something a little more formal for dinner with my parents tonight."

"Dinner with your parents tonight? Are you serious?" Simone's mouth fell open. "We don't even have a signed contract yet!"

"Consider it a test run." I grinned. "And don't worry. I'll send a cheat sheet along with the contract. Oh, and dinner's at eight sharp. I'll have my car come pick you up."

"But, Harry, I don't even—I mean, you don't even know where I live—"

"I'll see you at dinner, my lovely fiancée!" I offered her a quick wave, then turned my attention to my laptop, already pulling up a contract template.

5

SIMONE

I was wearing a little black dress in the back of a big black SUV.

Harry was sitting right next to me, wearing all black, too. It was almost like we'd coordinated our outfits, like we were the kind of couple who spent time organizing our closets together.

Good.

The more it looked like we were really a couple, the better.

"You wanted to major in philosophy in college?" I asked, scrolling through Harry's getting-to-know-him cheat sheet. "That's surprising."

"Wanted to but didn't." He shrugged. "I thought that learning about great thinkers would turn me into one, but I quickly discovered that hearing about Plato just made me desperate for a nap."

I laughed as I kept scrolling. "You used to live in New York?"

"NYU. It's where I got my master's in business."

"I'm surprised you didn't go to an Ivy."

"Why?"

"I don't know. I just assumed all rich people went to Ivies?"

"Columbia waitlisted me," he admitted with a grin. "You're right. I very much wanted to go to an Ivy. But I didn't want to wait another year to get started with grad school, either."

"Too much partying in undergrad, huh?"

"Better than always playing it safe, Ms. Goody Two-Shoes." He playfully quirked an eyebrow in my direction. "What about you? What are some things I need to know before dinner?"

"Nothing much. I already told you about my mom."

"But what about *you*, Simone? What do I need to know about you?"

"I really like my job and hope this whole contract thing doesn't negatively affect it?"

"Why are you doing that?"

"Doing what?"

"Keeping me at arm's length," he replied. "Keeping me all the way out."

"Honestly? There's just not much to know. I was born and raised in Los Angeles. Not the rich part, obviously." I lightly chuckled. "But it was still nice. I've always wanted to get into writing but I didn't know how. Before I started working for you, I was stuck in office job after office job. Mostly customer service."

"And then Taylor brought you to me."

"There you go. You've got the whole story." I sighed. "Stability's always mattered more to me than following my dreams. So, it's nice being able to do something that feels like it's just for me."

"Finally. Something real." He smiled. "Something about you."

I rolled my eyes even though I felt my heart suddenly racing behind my chest. He seemed more handsome than usual tonight, his black dress shirt outlining his muscular arms. It didn't help that we were in such close proximity that I couldn't get away from his scent, no matter how much I tried.

I was absolutely surrounded by Harry O'Donnell, in the very best and the very worst way.

"We should get our story straight, about how we met," he continued. "Do we want to go with the coffee shop story?"

"You mean, the fact that we literally met at a coffee shop? Because that's not much of a story."

"We can say it was love at first sight. Although, we should probably be vague about the timeline."

"Right, because getting engaged to a woman you met two days ago is less romantic than it is concerning."

"You get it." He chuckled, relaxing against his seat. "Fuck. I never know how I make it through these dinners, but I always manage to. Somehow."

"Please. How bad could dinner with your family be?"

"You'll see."

"I'll see what? A bunch of perfectly lovely people who love and support you?"

"Are you forgetting the whole reason you're here tonight? Because they're completely unreasonable people?"

"Wanting to carry on the family line isn't the worst thing in the world."

"How are you on their side when you haven't even met them yet?" He scoffed. "Or are you so anti-me that you'd be on anyone's side? As long as it isn't mine?"

"I'm not against you, Harry. And I'm not for your family, either. Not without meeting them first."

"Could've fooled me."

"I just think you don't always appreciate what you have. What you've been given. People would kill to be where you are."

"Only because they don't have the full picture."

"I think you're the one who doesn't have the full picture, Harry." I shook my head. "I don't think you know what it's like for people who don't just get to inherit a whole company."

"Are you seriously blaming me? For something I have no control over?"

"I'm not blaming you. I just think you could be more appreciative—"

"Mr. O'Donnell, we're here." Harry's driver had stopped the SUV in a driveway.

And when I looked out the window, I could hardly believe what I was seeing.

Whoa.

We'd parked in front of a huge mansion, the kind of place I'd only ever seen on reality TV featuring very wealthy and very catty housewives. The lawn was perfectly manicured, with a large fountain right in its center. There were also small lights illuminating a path to the front door, so long and so glamorous it could've been a runway in Paris.

My breath caught in my chest, even as Harry opened my door for me and took me by the hand.

"For what it's worth, I appreciate every single thing I have," he muttered as we walked down the path.

"Could've fooled me," I murmured his words from earlier right back to him.

There was a tension between us, our argument from the

car still simmering even as he rang the doorbell. But as soon as an older woman pulled open the door, the tension seemed to disappear into thin air.

Time to pretend.

"It's you! It's really you!" The woman's eyes went wide and she grabbed me around the waist and pulled me into a tight hug. "You're real!"

"Mom. Please." Harry groaned. "You're going to do permanent damage holding on to her like that."

"Sorry, sorry." She let me out of her embrace but kept her eyes on mine. "It just feels like a miracle."

Harry's mom smoothed down her clothes and went on. "I'm Grace."

"Hi, Grace." I smiled warmly. "I'm—"

"Oh, we already know who you are, Simone." Grace chuckled. "Well, we don't know everything. But I'm sure you can fill in the blanks over dinner."

An older man with graying hair walked into the foyer and gave me a warm smile.

"Hello, Simone," he said as he extended his hand to shake mine. "Jonah O'Donnell. We're very glad to meet you."

I shook his hand and smiled. "So nice to meet you both."

I swallowed. This was really happening. We were really pretending to be engaged. Had I gotten in over my head?

As I took in the beautiful surroundings of Harry's childhood home, I realized that I most certainly had.

Grace motioned for us to follow her deeper into the house. I reached for Harry's hand as we stepped into the living room, a silver chandelier hanging overhead. Everything inside the mansion was impossibly beautiful, with grand paintings lining the walls, exquisite art displayed on tables, and marble tile everywhere I looked.

When we reached the dining room, I took a seat next to Henry, quietly letting out a breath I didn't know I'd been holding.

"Are you okay?" he whispered.

"I'm fine. It's just... everything's new to me."

"Don't worry. They're going to love you." He smiled as he spoke.

I hastily forced the butterflies out of my chest. I didn't know what was going on with me, but I knew better than to let Harry get in my head.

Besides, we were all wrong for each other. Pretending to like him was one thing, but *actually* liking him?

That would've been a total mistake.

"There you are! Oh my God! You're real!" A young man who looked like Harry suddenly entered the dining room, already laughing. "Mom and Dad said Harry had a girlfriend, but I had to see it to believe it."

"Hey, Sean." Harry's tone was clipped.

"Hey, big brother." Sean slapped Harry on the back before taking a seat across from us. "How's my competition doing?"

"You really think *Front Stoop* can compete with *LA Now*?"

"I've always loved how humble you are, Harry." Sean smirked. "You've never been arrogant a day in your life."

"Can you two go more than five minutes without having a pissing contest?" A woman who looked like she was closer to my age took a seat next to Sean. She was gorgeous in an effortless way, and I wondered if she worked as a model.

"This isn't a pissing contest, Ruby," Harry corrected. "This is just your husband being delusional, as always."

"You boys and your magazine toys." Ruby sighed and threw me a wide smile. "I love your dress, by the way. It's very chic."

"Thanks." My words were shaking with nerves. "Were you—are you—a model or something?"

"In a past life. Yes." Ruby took a graceful sip of water. "But ever since having Maxon, I realized motherhood was my real dream."

She then exchanged a knowing look with Sean, one that was filled with love. He kissed her on the cheek in response, and she giggled and playfully pushed him away.

As I watched them, it felt like a knife was twisting in my chest.

I remembered when motherhood was my dream, too.

6

SIMONE

"So, Simone," Grace started. "How did you and Harry meet each other?"

Dinner had just started, with a medley of seasoned vegetables and fresh bread being placed on the table. I looked over at Harry, my mind suddenly going blank.

"I—uh—"

"We met at work," Harry smoothly answered the question for both of us. "Well, not exactly, but it was close enough. We actually ran into each other at a coffee shop."

"A coffee shop?"

"It's the one near *LA Now*," I said, my brain finally coming back online. "It's kind of a funny story. Harry was in a rush to get to work. So much of a rush that he cut ahead of me in line. He tried to order, but I stopped him. Told him that it wasn't fair to cut in front of people like that."

"Good on you, woman." Ruby grinned. "Men like Harry need more people standing up to them. Not less."

"Yes, I'm quite impressed by that story, too," Jonah joined the conversation. "Sounds like you two were a good match, right from the start."

"Is it awkward? Working together?" Grace continued. "I couldn't imagine working with my significant other. I feel like things at home would be so tense."

"It's not hard at all, really," Harry replied. "Who wouldn't want to see their favorite person all the time? I feel lucky that I get to see Simone so often."

I smiled at Harry's words, even though I knew they weren't true. It was still nice to think about someone who cared about me talking like that, even if it was never going to be Harry.

Not for real, anyway.

"Ah. He's completely smitten. That's the difference, Grace," Jonah joked with his wife. "They're still at that stage where they want to do everything together."

"Young love." Grace wistfully sighed. "I'm so happy for both of you."

I relaxed against my seat as I took a deep breath.

Phew. They were totally buying it.

And now we just had to get through the rest of dinner without any surprises.

~

"You're not going to have dessert?" I pressed as I took a bite of vanilla bean ice cream.

Harry shook his head. "Ice cream isn't good for the brain."

"Who cares about that? It's good for the soul."

"She's right, you know," Ruby chimed in. "Refusing ice cream can only lead to some very dark places."

"Yeah, yeah. Whatever." Harry gave in, sticking his spoon into my bowl. "If it gets you two to leave me alone, I'll take a little bit of brain damage."

"Simone, how in the world do you put up with his grumpy ass?" Ruby chuckled. "Seriously."

"I just take it a day at a time," I joked, then glanced around the table.

The rest of dinner had gone extraordinarily, suspiciously well, with Harry's parents seeming satisfied with our relationship. Sean and Ruby seemed to buy it, too. They were already kidding around with me like I was part of the family.

At first, I was confused by their warm reception, especially since Harry acted like spending time with them was such a chore. But as the night went on, I started to wonder if Harry was actually the odd man out.

And then I wondered what that must've been like for him, growing up in a family where you felt like you didn't belong.

How lonely that must've been.

"Everyone? I have something I want to say." Harry suddenly stood up from the table, and his family's attention flew toward him. "I, uh, I have an announcement."

He paused for a moment before he went on. "Simone and I are engaged. And we'll be getting married. Soon."

Grace gasped and placed a hand over her heart. "How soon?"

"Not so soon that we won't be able to send out invitations, I hope," Jonah said. "I do have a few colleagues who'd love to attend, but they'd need more notice than this."

"I'm sorry if my relationship doesn't take into account your work colleagues, Dad."

"Do you already have a dress picked out?" Ruby interrupted, her gaze landing on mine. "Wait. Do you already have a venue picked out?"

"I—um—" I started to sweat under the pressure. I was

also out of answers since Harry and I hadn't gone over any wedding day specifics.

Fuck.

The jig was up.

I began rehearsing an apology in my head for when Harry's family called us out.

"Simone is probably just as surprised as the rest of you," he continued. "In the past, I've been reluctant to commit to an actual wedding date but seeing her with you all now?"

He let out a deep breath. "It just hit me that I need to lock this down. This needs to be official between us. Because Simone belongs here. With you. With me."

Grace smiled over at me. "I think you're right about that, son."

"I'm your best man, right?" Sean joined the conversation. "I'm guessing it's either me or Paul, but Paul's not family."

"He's basically family," Harry shot back before he took his seat.

"Dad! Tell Harry that he has to make me his best man!" Sean said in a mock whiny voice.

Harry rolled his eyes and gave me a look as if to say, *See what I mean?*

As I took another bite of my dessert, I strangely felt more at home than I had in a very long time.

∽

"What was his house like? Did they have a bunch of rich people stuff?"

Taylor was on the other end of the line as I pulled a pair of jeans out of my closet. After dinner with Harry's family last night, we'd decided that he should meet my family, too.

Even if my mom was all the family that I had left.

"Oh, it was full of rich people stuff. Taylor, I could hardly process what I was seeing. Even their light fixtures looked like they cost thousands of dollars."

"What about his family? Were they nice to you?"

"The nicest." I held the jeans up to my frame as I looked in a mirror. "So nice that it was weird. He always seems so tortured when he talks about his family."

"Rich boy problems." Taylor laughed. "I still can't believe you're going through with this, though."

"Trust me. I can barely believe it myself." I threw the jeans back in the closet. "But if this helps my mom get that surgery she needs, I'll keep it up as long as it takes."

"Shit. Does your mom even know about all this?"

"Well, by the end of the night, she'll at least know that I'm getting married."

"Right. Good luck with that, babe." Taylor sounded like she was grimacing.

"Thanks for all your support." I chuckled as I walked back to my closet. "I'll keep you posted about how it goes."

It was the last thing I said before hanging up the call, my focus on the clothes I was laying out in front of me. A few moments later, I'd put together the perfect outfit–a bright, yellow sundress with a simple silver chain.

And a few moments after that, the doorbell rang.

I opened the door to see Harry standing there with a bouquet of sunflowers, the bursting colors matching my dress.

"You brought flowers?"

"Why do you sound so surprised?"

"It's sweet. Very formal." I took the bouquet into my hands. "I just thought you were more of a bad boy."

"Not when it comes to meeting moms." He smirked.

"When it comes to meeting moms, I'm the perfect gentleman."

"Apparently so." I motioned for him to come into the dining room where I'd set the table earlier. "Mom, come on! It's dinnertime!"

"I'm coming, Simone," she grumbled as her wheelchair appeared around the corner. "I don't understand what all the hubbub's about. Who's coming to dinner, anyway?"

She rounded the corner and stopped as she looked up at Harry.

"Hello," he said, reaching down to shake Mom's hand. "It's so nice to meet you, ma'am." He seemed nervous as he spoke.

"Mom, this is Harry O'Donnell," I said. "Harry, this is my mother, Eileen Didier."

"Oh. You're my daughter's boss?"

"Yes. And her fiancé."

"What?" My mom's eyes went wide and her mouth dropped.

The silence stretched out between us, and I glared at Harry. This was *not* how we'd planned to break the news to my mother.

"Since when?" Mom asked.

"Look, Mom! He brought flowers!" I showed her the bouquet in my hands, feeling nervous myself. "We should put them out on the dinner table, right?"

∽

*D*inner was so quiet I could've heard a pin drop.

My mom was being polite toward Harry, but not exactly warm. It was obvious that she was suspicious about why he was here and why we'd suddenly gotten engaged, and there was nothing I could do about those suspicions.

Not without breaking my contract, anyway.

"Those pork medallions were delicious, Simone," Harry said with a bright smile. "Seriously. I haven't had them that good in years."

"Thanks." I smiled back at him, even though I could feel my mom's gaze burning a hole through my head. "What about you, Mom? Did you enjoy dinner, too?"

"I did. Thank you, Simi."

"So, Eileen," Harry started. "Your daughter tells me that you were an amazing cook when she was growing up?"

"Yes. I was a pretty good cook. So I was told." My mom's response was dry.

Harry nodded, his eyes darting at me. "Would you both excuse me? I need to use the bathroom." Harry stood and hastily moved away from the dinner table. "Do you mind pointing out the way—"

"First door down the hall," my mom swiftly answered.

"Thanks, Eileen," Harry said as he disappeared from the room.

"Simi!" my mom whispered with a snap. "What's going on here?"

"What do you mean?"

"Don't play innocent!" she pressed. "You've either lost your mind or there's something you're not telling me. One minute, you're saying he's not your type. Then the next, he's telling me that you two are engaged? What the hell is this?"

"We're getting married so you can afford your surgery!" I blurted out the truth just as Harry stepped back into the room. I couldn't stand the idea of having to lie to my own mother about anything. "Harry needs to get married by his fortieth birthday to stay on as CEO of his family's company."

"So he's paying you? To get married to him?"

"It's a good deal for all of us," I sheepishly replied. "It's not like we couldn't use the money, Mom. And Harry's really good at his job. It's not fair if he has to step down just because he's not married in time."

"And you're telling me this handsome young man couldn't find a real wife of his own?"

"That's mostly my fault." Harry let out a small laugh. "I've been married to my job for a long time. I haven't done the best job in the romance department."

"I don't like this, Simone. I don't like this one bit." My mom frowned. "I think you should call it off."

"Mom, I can't just call it off. I already signed a contract, for starters—"

"You shouldn't have to do things like this for money. Or for me," she pleaded. "I want you to get married to someone because you love them. Not because you're trying to take care of me."

"It's already decided, Mom." I reached out toward her, resting my hand over hers. "Can you try to be supportive of me? Even if this isn't what you want?"

"I can try, Simi. I can try." She sighed, turning her palm up toward mine. "I just hope this goes the way you want it to."

7

SIMONE

*P*lanning a wedding in a week's time went about as well as could be expected.

Thankfully, I had a lot of help. Harry hired me no less than three wedding planners, who presented me with various choices I just had to sign off on. Still, it was a stressful experience. Especially since I hadn't seriously thought about getting married since I was dating Jace last year.

Since he broke my heart into a million pieces and just walked away.

"You look like a vision." Ruby was standing in front of me, eyeing my custom designer gown. "I can't believe Harry got this made for you in a week."

"Friends in high places, I guess."

"More like friends literally everywhere," Taylor joked as she handed me a glass of white wine. "Are you sure you're ready for this, Simone? Because I'm not, and I'm just going to be in the audience watching it happen."

"I'm ready. I love him." I sipped my wine as I looked over

at Ruby, hoping that she bought the lie. "I always knew that it was going to be Harry. Always."

"Such a fairy tale." Ruby sighed, followed by a smile. She then looped her arm around Taylor's. "Come on. We need to get to our seats. Let the bride finish getting ready for her big day."

"Okay, okay." Taylor's words came out anxious. "But Simone, I promise, if you need anything, even if it's a ride out of here, just tell me, okay? There's nothing wrong with being a runaway bride."

"Well, the running away part might feel problematic to Harry." Ruby chuckled as she pulled Taylor out of the room. "So let's try to stay put. Shall we?"

I weakly smiled as they disappeared out of my view.

What the hell was I doing?

Fake marriage or not, things were starting to feel pretty damn real. I hadn't considered just how much lying was going to be required in this arrangement, despite our whole relationship being based on a lie. I was genuinely worried that I was going to crack at any minute, ruining everything just because the guilt was eating me alive.

"Fuck." It was all Harry said when I finished walking down the aisle and turned toward him.

"Really?" I whispered. "That's all you have to say to your soon-to-be bride?"

"I think it's all I can say right now. You just look so incredible." His eyes widened like he was in complete awe. "You're beautiful, Simone. Please tell me that I've told you that before."

"First time for everything." I beamed back at him. "You clean up pretty good yourself."

"Did you write your own vows?"

"I was supposed to write vows?"

"Don't worry about it." He laughed. "I've got both of us covered. I'll just do mine and you can pretend like you're so overwhelmed with tears that you can't read the ones you definitely wrote."

"You wrote vows?" I was still shocked by the revelation. "But we barely know each other."

Before he could respond, the officiant began to speak. He went through the ceremony as Harry's mom gently wept in the front row. My own mom had a concerned look on her face the whole time, like she was waiting for the other shoe to drop.

When the time came for us to recite our vows to each other, Harry quickly volunteered.

"My dearest Simone," he started. "You're the light of my life. You're the reason I look toward the future with hope, which is new for me. I've got a reputation for being more pessimistic than most, but when I'm with you? I can't be cynical. I can't be anything other than in love with you."

He looked at me as he said the rest. "From the first moment we met, I knew that you were different from anyone I'd ever met before. You're honest with me, in a way few people are, probably because of said pessimism." He smiled, and a few people in the audience laughed. "And you're brave. I think because you've had to be, with everything that's happened in your life. I just wanted you to know that I see that bravery, and it makes me love you even more."

I swallowed a lump in my throat and wiped at my eyes.

Was I crying?

I knew that I was supposed to cry to sell the moment, but these weren't fake tears. Harry's words had managed to touch my heart, even if he didn't mean them. I'd never had someone speak about me like that before, and I obviously hadn't been prepared to hear it.

The rest of the ceremony was a blur of tears and celebration. We were pronounced husband and wife, and everyone cheered as Harry took me in his arms and kissed me.

That kiss was amazing.

I breathed in his scent, feeling dizzy as he pressed his mouth to my lips. I wanted to melt in his arms. I wanted him to never let go of me. When he pulled back, his eyes locked on mine.

And for a second, I thought maybe something was there.

Get it together, Simone. This is all an act. He's acting right now.

The next thing I knew, I was dancing at our reception, doing a conga line with Ruby, Sean, and Taylor. Then I was sitting at a table next to Harry, holding his hand, listening to Paul and Sean take turns telling embarrassing stories about him.

I was cutting into a slice of cake, with Harry's arm wrapped around my waist. I was kissing him, hard, in front of our family and friends, like the world was going to end if we didn't.

And even though none of it was real, the smiles were. So were the tears, and the happiness, and all the overflowing joy that took up so much space in the room it felt like we were swimming in it.

~

"Honeymoon suite, party for two."

Harry had just finished swiping his card at the hotel room door, giving us both access to the space. We were in a five-star hotel in Malibu. Harry's parents had insisted we take a honeymoon, even if it wasn't very far from home.

"Oh, wow." I was stunned as I looked around the room. "This place looks like it costs more money than I've ever made in my life."

"Courtesy of Mom and Dad." Harry set our suitcases down in the corner. "They pretty much demanded that they pay for our honeymoon. I tried to tell them that I make my own money, but they refused to take no for an answer."

"Tell them I said thanks!" I giggled, running toward the bed. I happily flopped down on the comforter before letting out a satisfied sigh. "Ugh. This is the most comfortable mattress I've ever been on in my life."

"Yeah? Let me know how it sleeps."

"What do you mean?" I squinted in confusion. "There's only one bed. Where do you plan on sleeping?"

"Right here." Harry patted the back of a nearby couch. "Or if it's too uncomfortable, maybe I can get a room next door—"

"Harry. Are you serious?"

"As a heart attack. Why?"

"We're both adults. We can share a bed without it being weird," I started. "Besides, if this whole marriage thing is supposed to look real, how are we going to explain it if someone decides to pop by and they notice that you're sleeping on the *couch*?"

"No problem. I'll just tell them that I prefer the couch."

"So, your plan is to scoop even more lies on top of all the lies we're already telling?" I scoffed as I waved him toward the bed. "Oh my God. Just come here. Lie down."

Harry did as he was told, eventually settling in beside me. He seemed tense, his arms folded across his chest.

"See? That's not so bad, is it?" I smiled.

"You're right. This mattress is pretty heavenly." He closed

his eyes as he spoke. "Much better than the couch would've been."

Even with his eyes closed, Harry still seemed way too rigid and tense. It was like he was seconds away from going into an important boardroom meeting instead of on his honeymoon.

Was he able to relax? Ever?

The thought of him spending the majority of his life all tensed up made me feel sad for a reason I couldn't explain.

"You can relax, you know." I playfully nudged him in the shoulder, trying to snap him out of his tense state. "I know you CEO types are usually in stress mode, but this is literally your honeymoon. The only thing anyone expects for either of us to do is have fun and chill out."

"And consummate the marriage. And produce an heir."

"Produce an heir?" I smirked. "I'm sorry, I didn't know that we were responsible for the future of the country—"

"You know what I mean, Simone. The whole thing about legacy and my family—"

"What happens if we don't produce an heir? Do I have to go live out the rest of my days at some faraway castle? Will the townspeople shame me for it?"

"Simone—"

"Are you going to cut off my head, Harry? If I can't produce an heir?"

Harry started to laugh. "Simone, be serious."

"Why?" I nudged him again. "Sure, your family is probably hoping that I pop out a baby in the next nine months, but you and I both know that's not going to happen. This isn't real, Harry. Which means there's no real pressure, either."

"Right. You're right." He let out a tired sigh. "We won't even be together in nine months, will we?"

"Nope."

"So, I don't need to worry about letting everyone down."

"Letting everyone down? You're going to do incredible things with *LA Now*. That's going to be your legacy." I shrugged. "You doing great things doesn't have to include marriage and kids. That's not everyone's path, anyway."

Harry smiled as he shifted closer to me on the bed. He then turned over so that he was on his side.

"You're so..."

"Rational? Practical? Correct about anything and everything?"

"Different," he corrected. "You're so different."

"Is that a good thing or a bad thing?"

"A good thing. I really don't think I've met anyone like you before, Simone."

"Oh, you probably have. I mean, I'm sure you've cut all kinds of people off while they were trying to get their coffee."

"You're never going to let that go, are you?" He laughed.

"And you're never going to apologize properly, are you?" I laughed now, too.

There was a quiet moment between us then, Harry's eyes slowly meeting mine. Something heated was behind his gaze, something that made me wonder what exactly was on his mind.

A pleasant shiver ran through me as I waited for him to move again, to say anything.

"If it's not real between us, shouldn't that mean that there aren't any consequences, either?" he asked quietly as he reached out a hand toward me.

Soon, his fingers were lightly trailing down the side of the dark green dress I was wearing. It was silk and expensive, an outfit that Ruby had insisted on gifting me for my honeymoon. My breath caught in my chest at his touch.

"No consequences?" I somehow managed the question even though I was extremely distracted.

"No consequences," Harry repeated, his fingertips now trailing down my stomach. "I want you, Simone. More than I've wanted anything or anyone in a very long time."

I tried and failed to think of something to say, as I felt Harry's palm casually slide between my thighs. He held his hand there, right over my panties, like he was waiting for me to give him permission.

And I quietly nodded, right before he slid his palm underneath the fabric.

8

SIMONE

"Harry..." I groaned his name as he circled my clit with his thumb. "Fuck..."

I gripped his shirt in my hand, pulling him even closer to me. His face was so close to mine now that he could've kissed me. Instead, he kept his gaze locked on mine, like he was studying my every move.

And then he slipped a finger inside me.

I groaned again, every inch of my body feeling like it was suddenly on fire in the very best way.

He fingered me deeper, his thumb still swirling across my clit as he did. My cheeks grew hot as I started to shamelessly moan. I was embarrassingly wet for Harry by this point, knowing full well that the sheets would be soaked by the end of the night.

I moved my head closer to his, my lips yearning to meet his own. He met me in the middle, his mouth crashing against mine. It felt like being in a storm. Whatever was brewing between us threatened to sweep us both away.

He pressed his tongue between my lips, just as he

slipped a second finger inside of me, filling me up to the brim.

"Harry..." I gasped as I wrapped my arms around him. "Fuck. I'm so close..."

My stomach clenched as an orgasm threatened to rip right through me, my body moments away from pure bliss. But just when I was on the verge of coming for him, I felt him move his hand away from me.

"What? Why?" I whimpered. "Are you teasing me?"

"That's not how I want you to come tonight." He shook his head as he moved down the bed.

"Because you don't want me to come at all?" I panted.

"Because I want you to come in my mouth." It was the last thing he said before he pulled my panties completely off, rolling them down my legs. A few seconds later, his face was buried between my thighs.

Fuck.

Harry wasted no time pressing his tongue against my clit. Each stroke of his tongue was perfect and precise, almost like he'd done this with me a million times before. I whimpered again as he tasted every part of me. His hands were pressed against my inner thighs as he held me wide open for him, giving him even more access to my pussy.

He slipped two fingers inside of me again, his mouth still flawlessly working my clit. And I felt myself beginning to break into pieces, my hips helplessly bucking against his tongue and fingers. I was practically riding his face, but I couldn't stop myself.

"Harry! Harry! I'm coming!" I cried out as I came, my pussy tightening around his fingertips, my clit still beneath his tongue.

I struggled to catch my breath as the final waves of pleasure rolled through me. I didn't even notice that Harry was taking off the rest of his clothes as he stood at the edge of the bed. When I finally looked at him, he was standing in only his boxers, his fingers tugging at the waistband.

My eyes went wide when I saw the size of his cock, the length of it soon bobbing free from the fabric.

"Take off your dress," he commanded. "I want to see all of you."

I nodded in agreement and pulled my dress over my head. I tried to be as graceful as possible while also moving incredibly fast. I was beyond ready for Harry to be inside of me, which was probably why I threw my dress and bra toward the other side of the room as soon as I was free of them.

When I was fully naked, I got back into position with my legs spread wide in front of him.

"Fuck. You're so fucking beautiful," Harry groaned as he settled between my thighs. His cock felt heavy against my clit. "Do you have any idea how gorgeous you are?"

I started to answer, but my words failed me as Harry pushed his cock into me. I moaned for him as he slid inside of me, not stopping until every inch had disappeared inside my pussy.

He then pulled my legs up on either side of his waist, keeping me in place as he began to thrust against me. His hips moved at a steady rhythm as he slid his shaft in and out of me, my body melting underneath his frame.

"Harry! Harry!" I called out his name as he fucked me, as another orgasm built inside of me. Almost like he knew what was on my mind, Harry shifted our position, moving my legs from his waist to his shoulders. As soon as he moved against me, this time much deeper than before, I felt myself coming for him.

"That's right, baby. Come on my cock. Just like that,"

Harry said as he moved even faster inside of me. "Fuck. I'm coming, too."

Harry kept fucking me, fast and deep, as we came together. It felt like lightning and thunder were flooding my veins, like every inch of my body was electric. I was lost in a world of bliss, stars blooming behind my eyes, even as his hips went completely still against my own.

"Fuck," he groaned, his fingers gripping my thighs as he came to a stop. "That was fucking... everything."

I tried to come up with something to say in response, but I was still lost among the stars.

9

HARRY

"Are you a breakfast person? Or more of a brunch person?" Simone asked as she held a room service menu up to her face.

She was wearing an oversized T-shirt with her hair tied back with a blue hair tie, so casual and so relaxed. There was nothing about her that hinted at what happened between us last night, almost like it hadn't happened at all.

"I'm guessing there are different menus for each option?" I tried to match her casualness, even though everything inside of me wanted to pull off her shirt and run my mouth across her breasts—

Nope.

I couldn't let myself keep going there. It was bad enough we'd slept together even once.

Throwing more gasoline on an open flame was only going to end in disaster.

"Yep. And the brunch option is way more boozy," she joked as she leaned toward me to show me the menu in bed. She smelled so incredible that my whole body tensed up, unsure of how to react. "I think they put alcohol in everything. Even the eggs."

"Are we just going to pretend like last night didn't happen?" I blurted out as I looked over at her. "Is that the game plan here?"

"Weren't you the one who said there shouldn't be any consequences?"

"Sure, no consequences, but shouldn't we at least have a conversation?"

"About what?" Simone quirked an eyebrow. "About how nothing we did last night matters? It's not like it can happen again, Harry. And it won't."

"You sound pretty sure about that."

"That's because I am pretty sure." She smirked. "We were just getting something out of our system. That's all."

"Okay. Got it. Sounds good." I faked a smile back at her, still unsure of the situation. "And what about protection?"

"Protection?"

"We didn't use any last night. Do we need to pick up some Plan B or—"

"Not necessary."

"Oh. Because you're already on something? The shot? The pill?"

"Not necessary because my body is the ultimate pregnancy preventer," she joked, but her laughter seemed hollow. "I have severe endometriosis. Which means it's pretty hard for me to get pregnant without some major surgery. And even if I did get the surgery, nothing's guaranteed."

"Oh." I hesitated, afraid to push the subject. "I'm sorry. That must be so hard."

"It used to be." She shrugged. "Now, it's just another fact of life. Not the best. Not the worst. Just a fact."

I stared over at her, trying my best to read her facial expression. But Simone wasn't giving me a thing, her features calm and unmoved. I couldn't tell if she was downplaying her emotions around pregnancy, or if she genuinely didn't care about it.

Hell, maybe she never had.

"Would it be awful if I admitted that I'm a little relieved?" I started.

"Because you don't have to spend forty bucks on Plan B?"

"Because I don't think I'm cut out for kids. Ever. Just the thought of them gives me nightmares."

"Really? Why?" She tilted her head to the side. "I didn't think you were the kind of guy who was afraid of anything."

"I'm not afraid of the kids themselves. I'm afraid of all that responsibility." I sucked in a sharp breath. "Kids would need so much from me, and I don't know if I'd ever be able to give them enough. Honestly, and this is going to sound awful, but I really don't think I'd ever be able to choose anything over *LA Now*. If my kid had a recital or something, they'd always come second. Always. That company is everything to me."

"Hmm." Simone set the menu down in her lap. "In that case, I think you're right. You're not cut out for kids."

"Ouch."

"I'm just agreeing with you."

"It's just the way you said it." I chuckled. "Like you didn't need to think about it at all. I think it's great you're self-aware about it. Seriously. Do you know how many people can't admit that to themselves? That they'd be bad parents?"

A bad parent?

Sure, I might've been overworked, but I never said anything about being *a bad parent*.

As Simone's words rattled around in my head, she went right back to reading over the menu. I was deeply annoyed by her comment, but I couldn't tell her that, not after saying that I wasn't cut out for kids.

What was I so annoyed about, anyway? Wasn't I the one who'd brought it up to begin with?

Still, the comment stayed on my mind, even as we shared an order of boozy eggs and cinnamon French toast.

~

"I've never been super interested in the beach," I admitted while I set out a blanket against the sand. Simone was next to me, lying out on a blanket of her own.

She was also wearing a hot pink two-piece, so much of her skin on full display.

A part of me wanted to see her without the bikini, of course. But another part of me wanted to offer her a coverup, like she was showing herself off when that part of her was only meant for me to see—

"What do you mean? Not super interested in the beach?" Simone's question interrupted my line of thinking. "But you're from Los Angeles."

"That doesn't mean I'm a beach person."

"Yes, it does! It means you're the prime example of a beach person!"

"I just never really got the appeal of it." I shrugged. "You sit outside all day and do what? Let the sun fuck up your skin?"

"You're supposed to be enjoying its rays. The warmth?" Simone's mouth hung open in shock. "You're talking like an alien right now."

"Ugh. Beach people. Always so obsessed with your precious sun." I pretended to hiss as I pulled sunscreen out of our bag, and Simone broke out into a laugh.

"Oh my God. You're completely ridiculous." She reached for the sunscreen and squeezed some into her palm.

She then held out her hand in front of me. "You want me to do the honors?"

"Yes. Please." I didn't hesitate, quickly pulling off my shirt. "When I try to do it myself, I always miss a few spots."

"Well, this is one of the perks of being married. Complete sunscreen coverage." Simone laughed again as she started to spread the sunscreen along my chest. Her cheeks turned red as she worked her way down my stomach, her fingers seeming to knead against my abs.

"You all right there? Or are you having flashbacks of last night?" I couldn't help myself.

"Nope. Never even crossed my mind." She handed me the bottle of sunscreen. "Your turn."

Her face was stoic as I rubbed sunscreen all across her chest, taking extra time under and around her breasts. But her façade started to crumble when I ran my fingers across her stomach, letting them get dangerously close to the edges of her bikini.

"Let me get your back!" Her tone was frantic as she yanked the sunscreen out of my hand.

A few moments later, we were lying next to each other underneath the sun.

"Did you ever build sandcastles as a kid?" she asked as she turned to look over at me. "I know you weren't much of a beach person but—"

"I supervised."

"Supervised?"

"Sean would build them and I would make sure they were up to code."

"That sounds like you had a little clipboard or something."

"I did. And a little highlighter, too." I grinned. "Our parents thought I was taking everything way too seriously, but Sean loved it. It made building sandcastles feel important."

"That sounds like such a good memory." Simone sighed. "It makes me wish I grew up with brothers or sisters. The closest thing I've ever had to anything like that is Taylor."

"That might've been for the best. The sweet moments are great, but the rivalry? The fighting? It can be pretty extreme."

"Is that why you and Sean aren't close anymore?"

"Who says we aren't close?" I chuckled again. "I think that's just how it is when you're brothers. There's always going to be some underlying competition."

"Especially when the family business is at stake."

"Exactly." I nodded. "How about you? Were you a sandcastle builder?"

"I supervised, too." She smiled. "My dad was the expert sandcastler. I just handed him the right tools and made sure the tide didn't ruin the whole thing. He made it feel like it was the most important thing in the world, being his right-hand girl."

"That sounds like a pretty good memory to me."

"It is." Simone looked away from me, suddenly focused on the waves that were lapping at the beach's shore. "How cold do you think the water is right now?"

"Probably pretty cold, but I have no intentions of finding out—"

"Let's go!" Simone shouted as she grabbed my hand, forcing me off my blanket.

"Hey! Hey! What the hell?" I protested as Simone pulled me toward the water.

But the big grin on her face was like a spell on me, and I let her pull me in.

"Woohoo!" she yelled triumphantly as the freezing cold water splashed against us.

"Fuck! Simone!" I quickly sucked air between my teeth. "That's so fucking cold!"

"But it's good, right?" She sank beneath the waves before popping back up. "It's so refreshing!"

"I think I'm going to freeze to death."

"Come on. All you need to do is get used to the temperature." Simone wrapped her arms around me, her chest pressed against mine. "Here we go!"

My eyes went wide as I realized what she was about to do. "Wait! Simone! No!"

But it was already too late. Simone and I were underwater together, her arms still wrapped around my waist, keeping me in place. When we came back up for air, we were both laughing like maniacs.

"I can't believe you just did that to me!" I gasped.

"I can't believe you didn't see it coming!"

"Why would I have expected that? Who brings someone underwater like that?"

There was more laughter between us, even as Simone swam into deeper water. I followed behind her with a huge smile on my face, the previously cold water now feeling so welcoming and warm against my skin.

~

"*Dance with me.*"

Simone and I had just finished dinner. We'd ordered one too many shrimp skewers and one too many drinks. Still, Simone seemed eager to get on her feet afterward, her hips already moving in time with the music that was blaring from the band on stage.

"Dance with me!" she repeated, her hand reaching for mine. "It's our honeymoon!"

"I don't think you can use that one," I said, even as I joined her on the dance floor. "I think that only works if it's *actually* our honeymoon."

"It might not be real, but it's real enough to dance." She rested her hands on my shoulders as she looked up at me. "Besides, we should have moments like this to look back on. Especially when your family starts asking us questions about what we did while we were here."

"You're right. This is good to have as a cover." I placed my palms on either side of her waist as the song changed to a slower number.

We swayed back and forth to the melody, perfectly matching the song's pace. Near the end of the song, I bent down to rest my forehead against Simone's, our lips so close to each other it was dangerous.

It might not be real but it's real enough.

I wanted her tonight, just as much as I wanted her last night. Maybe even more. I wanted to ask her if we could go back to our hotel room, if I could slip inside of her, if I could stay inside of her until dawn spilled in from the windows—

"I'm tired," Simone whispered as she moved her forehead away from mine. "I think I'm going to head to bed."

"I'll come with you."

"I mean it, Harry." She held up a hand. "I just want to

sleep tonight, okay? That's all. Just sleep."

"Okay, then. We'll just sleep."

I hoped to God she changed her mind.

10

SIMONE

"You look good in those sunglasses. You should get them."

I gave Harry a thumbs-up as we shopped at an outdoor market near the beach in Malibu. I'd suggested the idea after breakfast, since I figured getting a good walk in might help with the hangover we both had from last night.

Last night.

Ugh.

Thankfully, all Harry and I did last night was sleep. The problem was that I'd wanted to do so much more.

It was painful, having him that close to me in bed and not being able to touch him or let him touch me. The worst part was that I could tell he wanted me, too, with the way his stiff cock had pressed into my thigh practically all night.

"Are you sure? I'm worried they make me look too much like a beach person." Harry joked. "The last thing I want is people assuming I'm having a good time out here."

"If that's your concern, you should only wear them inside."

"Wearing sunglasses inside?"

"Yeah. I've seen people do it before."

"And were these people put on some kind of list? Because they should've been."

"So judgy." I chuckled before handing him a different pair of sunglasses. This time, the frames were heart-shaped. "What about these?"

"These are adorable." He took the sunglasses into his hand, then took a step closer to me. "But I don't think these would work on me. You, however..."

A few seconds later, he'd pushed a few strands of hair away from my face to make room for the sunglasses. He then gently placed them on my face. "There. Perfect. Just like you."

"You know, you're going to make some woman very happy someday." I beamed. "You always know just the right things to say."

"Some woman? Someday? What a strange way for my wife to talk." He laughed. "Careful. People might start to think this isn't legit."

I laughed, too, even as something roiled in my stomach.

This was a dangerous game, being with Harry like this. Even though I knew none of it was real and none of it mattered, sometimes it was too easy to forget that it was all pretend. And because I wasn't an idiot, I knew that if you pretended something enough times, it might as well be real.

But that couldn't happen with Harry. I couldn't let myself fall for him.

I wasn't his real wife, and I needed to remember that. Always.

Or else he was going to break my heart, just like Jace.

"Hey, are you okay?" he pressed. "You just got quiet all of a sudden."

"I'm fine. Sorry. I was just thinking," I said. I pointed over at a different stall. "Would you hate me if I wanted to go look at some wall art? Maybe find something to take home?"

"That depends. Is this the start of you redecorating my house?"

"Maybe." I playfully winked behind my shades. "We'll see how I feel when we get there."

Taylor: YOU SLEPT WITH HARRY??

Taylor: ARE YOU FUCKING ME?

Taylor: FUCKING *WITH* ME??

Simone: Definitely not fucking you or fucking with you!

Taylor: OMG WHAT HAPPENED? I THOUGHT THIS WASN'T SUPPOSED TO BE REAL.

Simone: Can you cool it with the all caps? You're stressing me out.

Taylor: Sorry, sorry.

Taylor: Okay. I'm calm now. What happened? Is there something going on between you two?

Simone: I don't know...

Taylor: You don't know? But you're fucking each other?

Simone: It was a mistake, I think. I'm not going to let it happen again.

Taylor: Or you *could* let it happen again? Maybe see where things go?

Simone: I already said it was a mistake, Taylor. If you make a mistake twice, it's not a mistake anymore.

Taylor: Whatever! I think you should just let whatever happens, happen.

Taylor: You're on your honeymoon, after all. 😊

Taylor: Which reminds me. Bring me back something cute! I'm so jealous of your fancy hotel life.

Simone: Next time I'll smuggle you in my suitcase. Promise. 😉

I was so grateful to be back in Los Angeles.

It felt like I was back in touch with reality, too, since the fake honeymoon was over. Harry was by my side as we took his car to my apartment, but whatever spell we'd been under while at the resort seemed to have been broken.

"I didn't approve any of those headlines, Paul," Harry said as he tucked his phone against his ear. "Right, so I don't understand why I'm seeing them live on the site. Did the writers' room do this? Or was it one of the managers?"

I happily sighed as I leaned against my seat. This was the Harry I was used to, all business, all the time.

Which was perfect, because there was no way I could ever fall in love with a guy like that.

"I'm not going to fire anyone. Who said anything about firing anyone? Just give me a name." Harry tapped on the glass divider, getting his driver's attention. "Did you get the flowers? Are they in the trunk?"

Flowers? What flowers?

"Yes, sir. They're in the trunk."

Harry nodded just as the car parked outside of my apartment. A few seconds later he'd hopped out of the car, walking toward the trunk. I followed him out, curious about what exactly was going on. Before I had the chance to ask any questions, Harry was thrusting a gorgeous bouquet of flowers toward me.

"For your mom. Again." He smiled slightly. "I think we

might've gotten off on the wrong foot last time. I'm hoping for a bit of a redo."

"That's really sweet, Harry, but my mom already knows what the deal is between us. You don't need to try to impress her—"

"I just want her to like me. That's all."

I playfully rolled my eyes before reaching for Harry's hand. We walked up to my apartment, soon knocking on the front door.

"Mom? Mom!" I called out as I tried to open the door. Realizing it was locked, I began to dig around in my purse for the key. "Weird. When she knows I'm on my way home, she'll usually leave it unlocked. Or just wide open."

"That sounds a little dangerous."

"For other people, maybe." I chuckled. "Trust me, my mom can handle herself."

"Maybe the caretaker we hired for her over the honeymoon started keeping the door locked?" he suggested. "I know your mom can handle herself, but it still seems like a safety hazard—"

"Simi?" My mom pulled open the door, her expression filled with confusion. "You're here? You're back?"

"You didn't get my texts?" I was confused.

"My phone didn't charge overnight." She motioned for us to come inside the apartment. "Willow didn't read through all of your instructions, I think, but she was still a lovely girl."

"She didn't keep your phone charged?" I tried and failed to hide how upset I was. "Mom, that's a really big deal. What if something happened to you while she was gone? What if you fell out of your chair or—"

"Nothing happened, Simi," she interrupted. "Everything's fine. See?"

I took a moment to look around the apartment, my rage boiling even hotter inside of me. It looked like Willow had done the bare minimum when it came to taking care of my mom, including leaving dirty dishes in the sink. There were also folded clothes resting on the couch, instead of in a closet or laundry hamper where they belonged.

"Yeah. It looks like nothing happened, all right," I murmured. "Mom, you have to tell me if someone's not doing their job—"

"Why? So, you can fly all the way back home and ruin your honeymoon?"

"It's not real, Mom. You know that." I frowned. "And you should also know that you always come first. Always."

"I didn't want to bother you for no reason, sweetie." My mom sighed. "Besides, Willow did her best. I think she just has too many clients to handle. I'm sure she'll do better next time."

"*Next* time?" I looked over at Harry, suddenly feeling desperate. "Harry, we can't leave my mom here like this. I know you want me to move in with you, but I can't just let someone else treat her like—"

"It's already handled."

"What?"

"I already took care of it." He nodded toward my mom. "Eileen, there's a guesthouse on my property that's being outfitted to support wheelchair use. It should be ready by now."

"Really?" My mom's tone was hopeful.

"Really." His smile was warm. "I'd be happy to have you live with us."

"That's..." Mom stopped and started. "That's so wonderful, Harry. Thank you so much for thinking of me. Thank you for letting me stay with my daughter."

"Of course. I'd never want to come between you two. Ever."

"I'm going to go pick out a few things to take over," Mom said, already motoring her wheelchair out of the room. "I think we still have that brown suitcase somewhere. I'll pull it out."

"Mom, hold on! I'll help you pack," I called out after her before turning my attention back toward Harry. "Thank you! Seriously. You have no idea how much this means to us."

I pulled Harry into my arms, instinctively hugging him. I was so thankful for his generosity in that moment that I'd forgotten about my own rules, about how much I wanted to keep him at arm's length.

I felt Harry hug me back, his arms tight around me. When we pulled away from each other, he was staring down at me, his dark brown eyes boring into mine. Without thinking, I leaned in toward him, so close our lips could almost touch.

But instead of pressing my mouth against his, I whispered, "I need to go. I need to help with the suitcase."

"Right."

"And I should really get my stuff packed, too, so I can get all moved in."

"Of course," Harry said, not moving an inch away from me. It was like we were frozen in place, moments away from falling into each other, moments away from making a huge mistake.

I took in a deep breath, finally moving away from him.

And I felt his eyes on my every move as I walked down the hall to find my mom.

11

HARRY

Fuck.

I should've kissed her.

I should've let her kiss me.

I should've done something other than just stand there like an idiot.

I was pacing up and down my living room as I kept replaying what'd happened back at Simone's house in my head, again and again. I was trying my best to respect what Simone wanted, but she was making it feel nearly impossible. If she wanted what happened between us to be a one-time thing, why did it seem like she wanted me just as much as I wanted her?

Or maybe that was the problem. She knew that we wanted each other, which meant that she also knew that we'd definitely end up in bed together. Again.

And that would've only led to more problems than we already had.

Simone was right.

When it came to being physical, we needed to stay far away from each other. The only path to peace was staying out of each other's mind and each other's bed. That way, we could continue with this sham marriage until it was time to call it off and there wouldn't be any hurt feelings or any harm done.

Besides, I wouldn't have known what to do with a woman like Simone, anyway.

I wasn't good at real relationships. And I'd never been good at love.

If any of this was real, I was only going to hurt her.

"Ooh, you look lost in thought." Simone beamed as she walked through my front door. "Are you thinking about firing someone?"

"Why does everyone think that today?" I shook my head in disbelief. "I'm not firing anyone. There's nobody's head on the chopping block."

"Not yet." Simone chuckled as she set a box down on a nearby counter. "Keep thinking on it. You'll come up with a name or two."

"Wait. Why are you carrying boxes?"

"Because my mom and I are moving into your house? And boxes make it easier to move things from one place to another?"

"No, I meant, why are *you* personally carrying boxes? I hired a moving service to help with that."

"They are helping. They're grabbing stuff out of the trunk right now."

"But the point is that they grab everything, Simone," I replied. "And all you have to do is tell them where to put things down."

"No, I get that. I just figured I might as well help out since I'm here."

"Unbelievable." I smirked. "I hope you know I'm not giving you a tip for this. I'm only tipping the crew I hired."

"I don't need a tip, but I do need to pick up a few things from the store after this." She pulled out her phone and began scrolling. "Mom wants to have a seafood dinner tonight."

"Sounds good. I can have someone come cook for us—"

"I can cook. It's not a problem," she cut me off. "I just want to make sure we have everything we need. You have spices, don't you? Black pepper? Salt?"

"Who doesn't have salt in their kitchen, Simone?"

"A man who can hire other people to do whatever he wants in the blink of an eye." She smirked.

"Touché."

It was refreshing to have dinner at home.

I'd rarely used my kitchen to cook, and even more rarely hosted guests for a meal. Dinner for me was usually hurriedly eaten at the office or while schmoozing with someone related to the magazine. It was barely a meal that registered on my radar anymore, although that'd been happening to the rest of my daily meals, too.

"Harry? Did you want another plate?" Eileen was smiling at me underneath the fairy lights on my backyard patio. "Simi makes such good salmon. Doesn't she?"

"She does." I smiled back at her, even though I felt like something was off between us. Eileen seemed so grateful for letting her live with us, but I couldn't shake how she'd responded the first time she'd learned about the arrangement between Simone and me.

"Mom, you don't need to stuff him. He's a busy man. He needs to stay limber," Simone joked before she took another bite of her steamed vegetables.

"I just wanted to make sure that he had enough to eat." Eileen innocently held up her hands. "And it's because he's so busy that I was checking in the first place."

"I might have room for another serving of salmon. We'll see."

I looked between Eileen and Simone. They shared a knowing look between each other, the kind of thing that develops between close mother and daughter.

The kind of thing I'd never be able to decipher in a million years.

"I'm really happy you're here, Eileen," I started, before my nerves had a chance to get the better of me.

"I'm happy I'm here, too." She flashed a small smile. "There's nowhere I'd rather be."

"But I just—" I tapped my fingers along the table, worried that I was coming at this all wrong. "Are you okay with me now? Are you okay with *this* now? Because when we first talked to you about it, you seemed pretty against it."

"Hmm." Eileen set her fork down beside her plate. "Well, if you really want my opinion..."

"Mom. Don't."

"He asked me, Simi. I think he wants to know." Eileen placed her palms flat against the table. "To be honest with you, Harry, I'm quite disappointed."

"Disappointed?" My heart started racing behind my chest.

Fuck.

Was Eileen about to take Simone back home? Was she about to blow up this whole thing?

"Don't get me wrong. Everything you've prepared for me to live here is perfect. And I can tell that Simi appreciates everything you do for her, too," she started. "But I always imagined that when Simi got married, it'd be the way it was between me and her father."

Eileen let out a tired sigh. "I just wanted Simone to be in love. That's all. I wanted to see her experience the pure joy of it. And honestly, I think she should've waited until she felt that way before getting married to anyone. And yes, I understand that what you two have is only temporary. Still, I wanted her to have the real thing."

"You've seen me have the real thing, Mom." Simone's voice was low. "And you saw the way it completely destroyed me, too."

"Jace wasn't the real thing, Simi. Which is something I tried to tell you—"

"It doesn't matter. It was real enough to me." Simone sounded like she was on the verge of tears. "It was real enough to break me and you know that. What's so wrong with trying something different? What's so wrong with not wanting to get my heart broken all over again?"

"Right. That's exactly right," I agreed with Simone. "What's wrong with not wanting to get hurt?"

"Ah. So, you've been hurt before, too?" Eileen asked.

"Uh, no. Not exactly." I shook my head. "More like, I never saw the point of getting too invested in a romantic relationship since I know how many of them end in flames. I'm not even sure if I believe in love, at this point, or if I ever did."

After I spoke, I realized my mistake, as images of my parents flashed through my mind, how happy they seemed throughout the years. I also thought about Sean and Ruby, how impossibly happy they were with their marriage, how they were still so in love even after all these years.

Maybe I did believe in love.

I just didn't believe that it could ever happen to me.

"A woman who's afraid of having her heart broken again and a man who doesn't even think he has a heart?" Eileen turned toward me, concern written all over her face. "Please, Harry. Just don't break my daughter's heart."

"You don't need to worry about that, Mom." Simone smiled. "Don't forget, there's nothing real between us. Harry could never break my heart because he's never going to have my heart."

It felt like someone had stabbed me right in the chest.

I tried my best to ignore the reaction, to pretend like it'd never even happened. But as the night went on, I couldn't stop thinking about it.

If I didn't even believe in love, then why did Simone saying she'd never love me make me feel so fucking awful?

12

SIMONE

"You could've been nicer at dinner." I helped my mom into bed, gently placing her against the mattress. "Harry's responsible for all of this, you know."

"I'm pretty sure I thanked him for everything, Simi."

"Yes, but you also made it known how opposed you are to all this." I sat down in the chair beside her bed. "Seriously, Mom. You don't need to be so—"

"Concerned about you?"

"So sure that this is going to blow up in my face," I corrected. "Or somehow end up ruining my life. Or breaking my heart."

"You're my daughter. Of course I'm going to worry about you."

"I know, Mom." I bent down to kiss her on the forehead. "Just worry about me a little more quietly? We don't want Harry calling this whole thing off before you even have your first surgery."

Mom waved a hand between us before she spoke. "Who

cares about the surgery? The only thing I care about is your happiness."

"Oh, you should definitely care about the surgery. Especially because I've already got you on the books with a spinal fusion specialist."

"Really?" My mom's eyes went wide. "You already booked me an appointment?"

"I got it booked on the last day of the honeymoon. We had a few hours during a layover at the airport."

"And? What do they think?"

"About what?"

"About my chances." Mom's voice started to shake. "Do they really think it would work? That I could get back some of my mobility?"

My heart broke for her in that moment. I suddenly remembered the flurry of doctors and surgeons we'd gone to right after the accident, when we were both still mourning my dad. It was a series of disappointments and tears, with doctor after doctor saying recovering her mobility was next to impossible.

But not anymore.

"They think there's a good chance, yes." I smiled down at her.

"And what about the side effects? What are the risks?"

"Do you really want to focus on that right now, Mom?"

"I just want to have all the facts." She pressed. "Is there a chance I could lose the little mobility I have left? What about the number of people who don't wake up after surgery?"

"Mom!" I groaned, completely unprepared to have a conversation this heavy. "Yes, okay, you're right. There's a chance you could lose the rest of your mobility, but it's extremely unlikely, okay? As in, if that happened, it's basically medical malpractice and we'll become multimillionaires overnight."

"And? What about the people who never wake up?"

"They're none of your concern."

"Because?"

"Because you're never going to meet them. Ever. So, you don't need to worry about what happened to them tonight."

"Simi—"

"Just don't, Mom." I reached for her hand. "Please don't make me think about what would happen if I lost you, too. I really don't think I could handle it."

She sweetly squeezed my palm with her own. "I understand, Simi. We should talk about something else."

"But not Harry."

"Who said anything about Harry?" She let out a breezy laugh. "I wanted to talk to you about your father."

"What about him?"

"Did I ever tell you how we met? When I was visiting Paris?"

"The rom-com." I laughed. "Yeah, I think I've heard this one before."

"I was just another confused tourist, completely lost. All I had was a guidebook and a few words of French in my back pocket. I bumped into your father at a beautiful café. I showed him my guidebook, stumbling my way through French. I was just trying to get to the Eiffel Tower, just like a million other people."

She grinned as she went on. "Of course, I assumed that a waiter at a café would be willing to point me in the right direction. Only, your father wasn't a waiter. Lucas was there on a date, a first date, with a woman he'd met the night before. Another tourist. But he always told me that from the first moment he saw me walk into that café, he knew he'd picked the wrong woman. And if he didn't at least try to get me in his life, he would've regretted it for the rest of his days."

"And so, instead of finishing his first date, he offered to show you to the Eiffel Tower himself," I said, finishing up the story. "But what he didn't count on was the girl from the café following you both over there. He also didn't expect her to explain what happened and how he'd ditched her to flirt with you. Which ended with her slapping him across the face—"

"—and me slapping him right after her!" My mom broke out into a full laugh. "He said his face hurt for a few days after that. But eventually, after some begging and pleading, he convinced me to give him another chance."

"I can't believe Dad was such a player." I smirked. "Two dates on the same day?"

"Lucas might've tried to be a player, but he wasn't any good at it." My mom wistfully sighed. "Your father was sincere to a fault. It was like he couldn't help himself."

Just then, her expression shifted into something somber. "That's what I'm so afraid of when it comes to you and Harry, Simi. I don't think he could ever give you anything like that. No sincerity. Nothing real."

"I'm not looking for anything real with Harry, Mom. I already told you—"

"I know you're not looking for anything real, but that doesn't mean it won't find you," she interrupted. "And I'm worried that if you fall for Harry, you'll never be happy. You'll never have the love story that you deserve."

"You worry too much, Mom. About the surgery. About Harry." I stood up from her bed with a warm smile on my face. "It's all going to be okay. Okay?"

"Whatever you say, Simi."

"That's the spirit." I offered her an energetic thumbs-up before I headed out of her room for the night. "Good night, Mom. Love you!"

"I love you, too."

~

"Oh. You're still up?"

I was holding a cold glass of water in my hand, after going for a late-night walk in Harry's backyard. His estate was massive and his lawn was well kept, which made it the perfect place to let out some of my restless energy.

My mom's words were still on my mind. Even though they were mostly unwelcome, they were still rattling around in my brain.

I know you're not looking for anything real, Simi, but that doesn't mean it won't find you.

"Yeah. I was just sort of pacing up and down the halls." Harry shrugged. "That's the benefit of having a house this big, I guess. Lots of space to get out some restless energy."

"What are you restless about?" I took a sip of my water, even though my eyes never left his frame.

"Nothing in particular. Just have a few things on my mind."

"Got it. CEO stuff?"

"Something like that, yeah." Harry's eyes were locked on mine. There was a familiar heat behind them, and something in my stomach clenched tight in response. Before I knew what I was doing, I felt myself moving closer to him.

Until I was standing so close to him that there was barely any space left between us.

"Hi." The greeting came out as a whisper.

"Hi back." Harry was still staring down at me but he didn't make another move, like he was waiting on something. "You should finish the rest of your water."

"Okay." I did as I was told, hastily drinking from the glass until it was empty. When I was finished, Harry gently took the glass out of my grip and set it down on the floor.

After that, he reached for me, pulling me into his arms.

His lips were on mine, his hands resting on the small of my waist. He was kissing me like he was on fire, like the world was going to explode in flames around us and this was our very last chance.

I kissed him back, just as fiercely, my fingers running through his hair, my arms wrapped around his shoulders.

I knew it was wrong, but I couldn't help it.

If I hadn't kissed him back, I would've regretted it for the rest of my days.

13

HARRY

I didn't know what came over me.

I knew I shouldn't have kissed her. I knew it was a complete mistake.

And yet, I couldn't help myself.

Even now, as I pressed my tongue into her mouth, all I wanted to do was be even closer to her.

"Hey! What are you—Harry!" Simone shouted as I suddenly picked her up and took her into my arms. "Where are you taking me?"

"I'm taking you to bed." I smirked at her as I headed toward my bedroom. "Husband and wife should at least be seen in their bedroom together sometimes, right?"

"Of course. This is for the sake of things seeming real." She smirked back at me. "Even though everyone who could see us is definitely asleep right now."

"There are always the security cameras."

"Smart man."

"That's what they keep telling me," I joked as I walked into the bedroom. I softly laid Simone down on the bed, then crossed the room again to close the door behind us.

"Is everything in your home this immaculate?" Simone pointed up at the ceiling. "I didn't even know they could decorate ceilings like that."

"Is that what you really want to talk about right now?" I grinned. "Because I can always give you the number of my decorative ceiling guy, if you're really that interested in it."

"Everything's just so upscale with you. It makes me feel like I'm playing a part in some fancy movie."

"Well, you *are* playing a part." I moved back over toward Simone and placed a hand on either side of her, hovering over her. "But I'm playing a part, too."

It was the last thing I said before I lowered my mouth to her lips, kissing her with just as much fire as in the hall.

She groaned underneath me, her fingers twisting into the collar of my shirt. I deepened the kiss between us as I started to grind my hips against hers. I wanted her to feel how much I needed her, pressing my hard cock against her thigh.

"Harry..." She moaned my name into my mouth as her hips bucked up into mine.

"Yes?" I tried to sound as innocent as possible even while I slid a hand between us, my fingers teasing her clit through her jeans. "Was there something you needed, Simone?"

"You're really going to make me say it?"

"Always."

"I want you," she whispered. "I want you, Harry."

"What do you want me to do?"

"Whatever you want."

"Whatever I want?" I shifted my hand from between her legs up to her shirt. I slid my hand underneath the fabric, soon finding her bra. I rubbed a thumb over one of her nipples, just as I started to kiss down the side of her neck.

"Fuck." Her voice was breathy as I pushed her bra even further up her chest, giving me full access to her breasts.

I took one of her nipples into my mouth, then my tongue circled the sensitive nub. Simone writhed under me, moaning with approval. I reached toward her other breast, my hand finding her nipple and rolling it between my fingertips.

"Harry. Oh my God..." She opened her legs underneath me, and I settled into place on top of her, my mouth and hand still working her chest.

I felt her shamelessly grinding her hips against me as I played with her. Even her moans changed pitch, getting louder, higher, and more desperate with each passing second.

"Harry, wait—if you don't stop, I think I'm going to—" Simone tried and failed to warn me of her oncoming orgasm, but I could tell it was already too late. A few seconds later and she was shivering underneath me, her breaths coming so much faster than before.

"Seriously?" Her cheeks went red as she covered her face with her hands. "I can't believe I just came like that. We were barely even—that's so embarrassing—"

"It's embarrassing that you want me inside of you?"

"It's embarrassing that you barely have to touch me," she said through her palms. "It's way too easy for you to—Harry! Fuck!"

While Simone had been overanalyzing our interaction, I'd pulled down her pants and panties, not stopping until they were on the floor in a heap. I spread her thighs wide enough for me to stick my head between them, casually thrusting my tongue inside of her.

"You're right. You are pretty turned on right now," I murmured before I tasted her again, playfully running my tongue along her sensitive clit. "You're so fucking wet for me, baby."

"Are you trying to embarrass me even more?" Simone whimpered before the sound turned into a guttural moan. My playfulness near her clit had turned serious as I made firm circles against it.

Fuck.

I loved the taste of her, loved the way she pressed her hips against my mouth.

I grabbed her thighs, keeping her in place as I continued eating her out, wanting to make sure she felt every movement of my tongue and lips. It wasn't too much longer before she came for me again, her thighs quivering as her clit throbbed against my tongue.

Fuck. Fuck. Fuck.

I was going to lose my mind if I wasn't inside of her right now.

I pulled off the rest of my clothes as I stood at the end of the bed. Simone seemed to be watching my every move, all of her attention on me as her breaths were shallow and quick.

"Turn around. Face the headboard," I instructed. "Get on your hands and knees."

Simone nodded before she moved into position, her ass in the air for me a few seconds later. I moved into position behind her, too, my knees sinking into the mattress. I placed one hand on her waist, then I used the other to slowly guide myself into her perfectly tight pussy.

She shivered when I was fully inside of her, just as I reached for her waist. I began to move my hips back and forth, sliding in and out of her at a steady rhythm. It was heaven being inside of her like this, my cock throbbing harder with each thrust.

"Harry... Harry..." Simone moaned my name, her hips moving back to meet mine. "That feels so good..."

"You feel so good, too." I picked up the pace, thrusting inside of her even faster than before. "You have no idea how fucking good you feel, Simone."

"Let me know when you're close..."

I nodded in agreement, just as my cock slammed inside of her again. I reached a hand between us, my fingers finding her clit as I continued fucking her deeper and deeper. Her pussy started to tighten around my cock and I knew that she was on the verge of coming again. Eager to push her over the edge, I started moving even faster against her, my fingers moving even faster, too.

"I'm close, baby," I groaned. "I'm so fucking close. I'm going to come so deep inside of you—Simone?"

She was moving away from me, shifting toward the front of the bed.

"That's not how I want you to come tonight." She smiled and motioned for me to lie down on the mattress. "I want to be on top of you."

"Works for me." I grinned right back and moved to lie down, my eyes never leaving Simone. "Get over here."

She lightly chuckled before she got into position on top of me, her knees resting on either side of my waist. She lowered herself onto my cock and placed her hands on my chest for balance. After that, she started to steadily grind her hips back and forth, my cock sinking so deep inside of her pussy.

"Fuck. Simone. Fuck." It was all I could say as I melted underneath her, my cock way too close to exploding inside of her. "Fuck, I'm—"

"Wait for me," she pleaded, her hips still grinding against mine. "I'm almost there, too."

I groaned as I reached for her hips, pounding my cock into her at an unrelenting pace. She gasped as I felt her pussy tighten around my shaft again, her orgasm quickly tearing through her. I was coming now, too, my cock filling her with my cum, my fingers gripping her skin tightly.

And then, when all was said and done, Simone collapsed right into my arms.

~

I wasn't supposed to be holding her.

Hell, I wasn't supposed to be fucking her either, but it seemed like that was already out the window.

Simone wasn't saying much. Actually, she wasn't saying anything. She was just staring up at the ceiling as she rested her head on my chest. She felt so far away from me mentally, even though she couldn't have been closer physically.

"Was that as good for you as it was for me?" I tried to bring her back to the moment between us. "Because I don't think I've ever come like that before—"

"I should get back to my room."

"Wait. What?"

"It's late." She casually rolled away from me. "I should get to bed."

"Really? Just like that?"

"Unless there was something you wanted to talk to me about?" Simone quirked an eyebrow. "Like for work or something?"

I tried to come up with something that would make her stay just a little longer.

But after a few seconds of awkward silence, I finally gave

up. "Nope. There's nothing I wanted to talk to you about. You're free to go."

"Cool. See you tomorrow." Simone smiled before she left my bedroom.

"Yep. See you tomorrow," I said to myself as I offered her a goodbye wave she never even saw.

14

SIMONE

I couldn't get to sleep no matter what I tried.

I knew that hooking up with Harry *again* was a total mistake. So, why couldn't I stop myself when it was happening?

And why had it been so hard to leave his room after it was done?

"It's not going to happen again. It's never going to happen again," I muttered as I pulled the covers over my frame for the millionth time in my bed at Harry's house.

I'd been going back and forth between settling underneath them and pushing them toward the edge of the mattress. "That was it. That was the last time. And now, it's done."

Great. I was talking to myself now.

I closed my eyes tight and tried to force myself to sleep.

But nothing was happening, no matter how many sheep I counted.

Maybe I just need some fresh air?

I looked over at the door that led to an outdoor patio from my room. There was moonlight spilling across the floor, making it look like a set from a stage play of *Romeo and Juliet*.

Before I knew it, I was standing on the balcony, with fresh night air blowing across my skin.

"Yep. This was exactly what I needed," I said, resting my hands on the balcony ledge. "I just needed some peace and quiet—"

"Are you on the phone with someone?" Harry's voice immediately interrupted my newfound peace and quiet.

And I moved back from the ledge, startled by his presence. When I looked over, I saw that Harry was standing out on his own balcony. Of course, his was a lot bigger than mine, with expensive-looking stone decorating its sides.

"Nope. Just talking to myself," I admitted. "Sorry if that's weird."

"Not weird. Especially since you probably thought you were alone."

"So, I'm guessing you couldn't sleep, either?"

"Not really. No." Harry let out a sigh before his eyes met mine. "Just have a lot on my mind, I guess."

"Me too."

There was silence between us then, but Harry never took his eyes off me.

"Simone?"

"Yeah?"

"Who's Jace?"

"Jace?" I blinked a few times at the question. "How do you know about Jace?"

"You mentioned him tonight. When you were talking to your mom," he said. "You brought him up when your mom was talking about having something real."

"Oh. Right." I nodded before I went on. "Well, Jace is —was—"

I struggled to speak, as the memories came back to me like a flood. "Jace was the man that I thought I was going to spend the rest of my life with. We were together for three years. We made all these plans. Talked about having a family. I really thought he was the one. I was more sure about Jace than anything else. Ever."

"What happened?"

"I couldn't have kids. That's what happened." I let out a hollow laugh. "It turns out, without kids, Jace wasn't interested in the rest. We tried to make it work for a little bit after we found out, but I could tell he was already gone mentally. And then, one day, he really was."

"Fuck. I'm sorry, Simone. That must've been so hard."

"Oh, it was awful. But you know what they say."

"What?"

"What doesn't kill you makes you wish you were dead."

Harry laughed as he shook his head. "Damn, Simone. That's pretty dark."

I laughed, too. "Sorry. Making jokes about it helps sometimes." I smiled as I turned the questioning on him. "And? What about you?"

"What about me?"

"You ever met anyone who broke your heart? Who got your hopes up just to let you down?"

"Not really." He hummed. "I mean, I don't think I ever really got that serious with anyone."

"Surprise, surprise." I teased. "Of course, you've never had anything too serious. You're already married to *LA Now*. And the last time I checked, people frowned on dating around when you're already in a committed relationship."

"It wasn't always my choice."

"Not always your choice?"

"Not being serious." Harry faintly smiled. "There was

someone. Once. Who I thought really could've been the one."

"But?"

"But she wasn't interested in going down that path with me. She didn't want anything serious. She just wanted to travel around the world together, basically as friends with benefits, from now until the end of time."

"That sounds amazing and awful at the same time." I frowned. "Spending all that time with someone you love but none of it really meaning anything? That would be torture."

"It was." Harry shrugged. "Which is why it didn't last too much longer after she told me that. Being with her did teach me a lesson, though. Something I'll never forget."

"And what lesson was that?"

"That I'm never going to have what my parents have. That I'm never going to have that once-in-a-lifetime fairy-tale kind of love. The kind you tell strangers about, just because it's such a good story."

"The kind you tell your kids about," I added, even though it was a little painful to say. "Honestly? I don't think I'm ever going to have that, either. My parents had a love story that's completely out of this world. I don't think that sort of thing happens anymore."

"Then what's the point of even trying? Why would we drive ourselves insane chasing after something that we know is never going to happen for us?"

"You're saying it's better to not even try at all?"

"I'm saying that if all we can get is a half-assed version of a beautiful love story, why bother?" Harry looked at me. "We could save that energy for something else. Something simpler. And we can keep our romantic commitments clean and quick."

The Wedding Hoax

There was something suggestive in Harry's tone, his eyes still on mine.

"I think we're on the same page about that." I smiled at him. "About keeping things simple. About keeping things clean and quick."

"Good. I'm glad to hear it."

~

"I think you left your panties in my bathroom," Harry whispered as he passed behind me in the kitchen.

I'd been living with him for a week now, and nearly every night I'd ended up in his bed. I knew that it was a horrible idea, but ever since our balcony conversation, it felt like Harry and I really got each other.

Or at least, it *seemed* like we did. We never talked about hooking up, despite the fact that we'd been going at it for days.

Should we be talking about it?

Or would that ruin the whole mood?

"I'll check on that later," I replied to Harry, who was now standing by my side. He was shirtless, his abs glistening with sweat like he'd just come back inside from a jog.

"I think you should check on it now. We don't want things to escalate." Harry slid his fingers underneath my shirt, his fingertips resting on my stomach. "What's going to happen if all your panties end up in my bathroom? That could be a national emergency."

"I don't think you know what counts as a national emergency." I laughed before I looked up at him. "Is this a flimsy excuse to get me into your bed again, Mr. O'Donnell?"

"Who said anything about my bed? I was talking about the bathroom, Mrs. O'Donnell."

"Ah. Of course. I'll just grab my clothes out of your bathroom and pretend your bed doesn't even exist, then."

"Hold on. I don't think anyone said you needed to pretend my bed doesn't exist—"

"Simi?" Mom called from the other room. Harry and I suddenly moved away from each other, now almost standing on opposite sides of the kitchen.

"Never mind!" she called out again. "I found what I was looking for."

Harry and I moved closer to each other again, and he held me for a moment.

He placed a playful kiss on my forehead before he winked down at me.

"I'll see you tonight, Mrs. O'Donnell?"

"That's likely, Mr. O'Donnell. Very likely."

I smiled at him as he left the kitchen, the expression on my face soon fading.

What are we doing with each other?

Whatever this was, it was starting to feel a little too real. It wasn't like I could resist him, either, which was making things feel even more complicated.

Crap.

I needed to get a grip on whatever this was between us, or else I was going to lose myself in it.

And if I lost myself in Harry, I didn't know if I'd ever find my way back.

15

HARRY

Things were starting to feel a little too real.

I knew it was a problem, but I didn't know how to stop it. Simone felt too good in my arms, in my bed, in my shower. I couldn't deny that I liked having her everywhere, even if things between us weren't going anywhere.

Even if she was going to be my ex-wife in a matter of months.

"Harry! You still there?" Sean groaned on the other end of the line. "I've told you about upgrading your phone. You're rich enough to—"

"My phone is fine, Sean." I rolled my eyes. "Why were you calling me again?"

"I was calling on behalf of Mom."

"On behalf of Mom? Why didn't she just call me herself?"

"Is that Harry? Harry, honey, I'm right here!" My mother's voice was suddenly on the phone. "Hi, honey. How have you been?"

"Mom, why are you communicating through Sean? Is there something going on that I should know about?"

"Yeah, it's because I'm her favorite kid! Duh!" Sean piped up in the background.

"No one's communicating through Sean, honey. I just told him to give you a call."

"Got it. What's up?" I folded my arms in pure frustration, waiting for someone to finally answer my question. "Why are you guys calling me?"

"We just wanted to invite you and Simone to brunch," Mom replied. "We thought it'd be lovely to have you. Oh, and of course, we'd love for Eileen to come, too."

"Is that even possible?"

"What do you mean?"

"Mom, you know Eileen is in a wheelchair," I reminded her. "Would she even be able to come over to the house? I don't think she'd be able to navigate the steps—"

"Don't worry about any of that, honey!" Mom assured me. "We've already taken care of it. We've had ramps put in and we had the house looked over for accessibility."

My heart dropped to my stomach.

They're revamping the house? Just for Eileen?

For a marriage that's not even real?

"Mom, you shouldn't have done that," I said, trying to backtrack. "I mean, you shouldn't have made any permanent changes to the house. I'm sure that was an unexpected cost—"

"What are you talking about, Harry? Eileen's family now. We care about her needs, too."

No, she's not. Eileen's not part of the family, and she never will be.

The words were threatening to come out of my mouth just as Simone stepped into my bedroom.

"Is that your mom?" She pointed at my phone. "What's going on?"

"Simone! There you are!" My mom's voice lit up as she shouted to be heard by Simone. "I was just inviting you and Harry over for brunch. Your mother should come, too!"

I tried to signal to Simone that we shouldn't go. I quickly shook my head, even mouthing the word "no" with a desperate flair.

"That sounds wonderful!" Simone said into the mouthpiece. "We'll be right over." She beamed at me and offered a thumbs-up, as if we were on the same page.

"Yeah. Yep. We'll be right over," I said into the phone, my heart still firmly in my stomach.

I ended the call and pocketed my cell, following Simone out of the room.

"I'm sorry, does shaking my head mean something different to you than the rest of humanity?" I said to her in the hallway. "Is today Opposite Day? Do I need to check my calendar?"

"No, but you need to think about how things look. A happy couple turning down a brunch invitation? That doesn't seem so happy to me."

"We could've said we already had plans."

"And what if your mother wanted to come over and drop off some food from brunch?" Simone pressed. "And she found us here, just hanging out on the couch?"

"That would've broken her heart," I admitted.

"Exactly. And it makes us liars, which is a pretty bad look if we're trying to convince people that we're happily married."

"Fine." I sighed. "You're right."

"Always am." Simone grinned as she stepped into the kitchen.

"So modest, too," I chimed behind her. Eileen was

already sitting behind a table, her hands folded in front of her.

"Good morning," she said, noticing Simone's smile. "You look like you got good news, Simi."

"I just found out that we're all going to Harry's family's place for brunch."

"Ooh. An invite to the mansion." Eileen smiled even wider. "I never thought I'd get the chance to go to the ball."

"Just let me make your protein shake, and then we'll get ready to go, okay?"

"Do I really need my protein shake if we're going to brunch?"

"You need your protein shake every day, Mom. Doctor's orders."

"Fine. Sure. Doctor's orders." Eileen blew out a sigh. She then turned her attention toward me. "You don't look as excited as she does, Harry. You don't like visiting your family?"

"I wouldn't say that." I took a seat next to her at the kitchen table. "Who doesn't like visiting their family? I'm not a monster."

"I didn't say you were a monster. You just looked a little hesitant." Eileen shrugged. "I was just wondering about it. That's all."

"It's complicated."

"Complicated how?"

"Complicated as in they're the whole reason Simone and I are doing this marriage in the first place," I answered. "Complicated because if they just trusted me to run the company without needing me to be married, I never would've gone through with any of this."

"Ah. So, this is a tradition in your family, then? Getting fake married to stay in charge of the family business?"

"Nope. Everyone before me got married of their own choosing. Long before their fortieth birthday, so the rule never had to be enforced."

"Have you ever told them how you felt about the tradition?"

"All the time." I leaned back in my seat. "But no one ever listens to me about it. They just bulldoze over me until I get in line with whatever they say."

"That's funny."

"I don't see what's so funny about it."

"Well, it's funny because you don't seem like the type of man who'd ever let anyone bulldoze over him," Eileen replied. "And yet, with your family, it's like they know just how to press your buttons."

"Isn't that how it always is?"

"I think so." Eileen smiled. "But they can't be all bad. Or else, you wouldn't still be dealing with them."

"That's because I've gotten used to them. They've always been like this, expecting way more from me when I'm already giving them everything I have. Their standards for me have always been impossible to reach. I think they did it that way so that I'd always be in overachiever mode—"

"But instead, it made you feel like you could never make them happy." Eileen finished my thought for me. "They wanted an overachiever but they got someone who's never satisfied."

"Except for the magazine," I added. "With the magazine, I'm completely satisfied with my work. It's the one thing that I know I'm doing perfectly."

"Which is why your family trying to take it out of your hands drives you crazy." Eileen hummed. "I think I'm getting the full picture now."

"You are?"

"I am." Eileen offered me a bright smile. "You're not that complicated, you know. I mean that in a good way."

"It's just—I kind of got the feeling you hated me."

"I don't hate you, Harry." Eileen shook her head. "Trust me. There are very few people that I hate, and you've never made it on the list."

I smiled. "That's a relief."

"And that's quite a compliment," Simone said as she set a protein shake in front of Eileen. "You should hear her talk about the butcher shop guy. He's definitely on her shit list."

"It's not my fault that he always weighs the meat wrong and ends up stiffing us."

Simone laughed, and she and her mother exchanged a knowing glance.

My heart ached at their connection as I thought about how complicated things were with my own family.

Why was it so easy for Simone and her mom to be this close?

And why was it so hard for me to be close to anyone?

16

SIMONE

"Uncle Harry! Come play catch with me!" A boy with a gap in his teeth was holding out a baseball for Harry to take. He couldn't have been more than six years old.

This had to be Maxon.

I hadn't had the chance for a proper introduction at the wedding, since Maxon had gotten tired and fallen asleep at his family's table. Now that I was finally up close, I could tell that he looked like the perfect mixture between Sean and Ruby, sharing all their features in equal measure.

Harry took the baseball from Maxon before he pointed toward the backyard. "We can play after brunch. I promise, okay? But I think your parents want us to eat brunch with everyone first—"

"Come on, Uncle Harry! Please!" Maxon begged. "Please! I never get to see you!"

"I think you should go play catch with him." I playfully nudged Harry in the shoulder. "If anyone asks where you are, I'll cover for you."

"Are you sure? Dealing with my family while I'm around is one thing. But tackling it solo—"

"I'm not solo, remember? I have my mom here, too."

"Maxon! You look like you've grown a foot since the wedding," my mom cooed at Maxon. She then looked over at Harry. "Harry! Go play catch with this young man at once!"

"Yes, ma'am." Harry smiled, then turned to Maxon. "Come on. Let's go hide out in the backyard before anyone notices that we're gone."

"Yay!" Maxon cheered as he followed behind Harry.

"He's a good kid. I can tell," my mom said as we made our way further into the mansion, moving up the ramp. "And he seems so sweet, too."

"He has good parents." I smiled down at her. "Sean and Ruby are doing a really good job with him."

"My ears are burning!" Ruby appeared in front of us with a glass of white wine in her hand. "Simone! So happy you could make it!"

She pulled me in for a tight hug, then did the same with my mom. "And Eileen! You are a vision, as always."

"Oh, please. Says the supermodel." My mom laughed. "You look gorgeous, Ruby. Like you just walked off a movie set."

"Where are you two sitting? Please say it's next to me." Ruby took a sip of her wine.

My face twisted with confusion. "Were we supposed to get place cards or something?"

"Nope. No place cards. Just seating preference." Ruby smirked. "Come on. Let's go snag a place at the table before the boys get all the good seats."

∽

From where I was standing, there weren't any bad seats at the table.

The dining room had been decorated like an upscale restaurant, with flowers hanging from its ceiling and printed menus in front of each seat. Even the drinks looked fancy, with bottles of expensive wine standing in the middle of the table.

"Simone!" Grace greeted me as soon as we walked into the room. "And Eileen! I'm so glad you both could make it."

She paused for a moment, glancing around. "Would either of you happen to know where Harry is?"

"He's, uh—" I started and stopped, just as Harry stepped into the dining room. "He's right over there, actually."

"Hi, Mom." Harry waved.

"And? Where were you?"

"Playing catch with Maxon." Harry beamed at Grace before he looked over at Ruby. "He's getting really good. I think Sean should really think about putting him on a team—"

"You were almost late." Grace sighed as she cut Harry off. "Let's all go sit. Ruby, you're next to me."

"It's an honor and a pleasure." Ruby smiled before she motioned for Sean to follow her over. Sean had been huddled in the corner of the room with Maxon, seemingly cleaning some dirt off his son's shoes.

I watched Harry's excitement deflate as Ruby and Grace walked away, and something inside my heart twisted at the sight.

Jeez.

He'd been excited about something, and it was like it didn't even matter. I didn't know if Grace had done it on purpose, but she'd snuffed something out in Harry before it even had a chance to shine.

When I'd first met Harry's family, I could tell he was the odd man out, but I still couldn't fully understand why he was so weird about them.

Suddenly, I had a clearer view.

"Should we go sit down?" I asked him as I took his hand. "And is there a right answer and wrong answer to where we're supposed to sit?"

He let out a small laugh. "Did Ruby try to tell you that? That's been one of her conspiracy theories ever since her first family brunch."

A few moments later, Harry, my mom, and I were seated across the table from the rest of Harry's family. Harry poured a glass of wine for each of us as I looked over the menu, my mouth watering at each item listed. I'd have to ask Harry later why his parents had menus at a family dinner at home.

"Do any of them know?" my mom whispered to me as she stared at her menu, too.

"Do any of them know what?"

"The truth. About you and Harry."

My eyes went wide before I whispered back, "No, Mom. They don't. And please don't say anything. This whole thing blows up in our faces if they find out—"

"I wasn't going to say anything. Don't worry—"

"Eileen, I've heard a rumor," Grace started with a wide grin.

My mom and I exchanged quick, nervous glances. I screamed internally.

Is this really about to happen right now?

I braced myself for impact, grabbing Harry's hand

The Wedding Hoax

underneath the table. If we were about to be called out by his whole family, at least we were together—

Even though we weren't together. Not really. Not at all.

And after Grace exposed us to everyone, we'd probably never talk to each other again.

My heart sank at the realization, my hand on top of Harry's now feeling uncomfortable and cold.

"A little birdie told me that you love flowers," Grace continued. "Is that true? Because I love flowers, too. And gardening. I swear, all I need to be happy in this life is my little garden—"

"I love gardening, too!" my mom said, a little too loud. It was obvious that she was relieved. "Or I used to, before the accident. I still tend to the plants that I can, though, and it brings me so much joy."

"We should work on a garden of our own." Grace smiled. "I've always wanted a gardening buddy. No one else ever wants to see to my plants with me."

Phew.

I let go of Harry's hand underneath the table. "That sounds wonderful," I said. "I can't wait to see what you two come up with."

"Harry? How are things at *LA Now*?" Harry's dad asked. "Still going good, I assume?"

"Do I ever give you a reason to doubt it?"

"I'm just checking in, son." Jonah nodded and grinned. "And I'm glad that you're still piloting the ship. I was starting to sweat when I thought Sean might actually get a crack at the wheel."

"Hey! What the hell?" Sean scoffed. "I would've been great as CEO."

"I love you so much, baby. But no." Ruby frowned. "Harry was born to run *LA Now*."

"It's true, Sean." Grace sighed. "Harry is the best at what he does. We couldn't ask for a better successor for your father."

"I actually think Harry would be great at whatever he does. CEO or not," I chimed into the conversation, unable to help myself. "He's really talented and he's so smart, you know? He'll always land on his feet. He's just too good."

What was I doing?

Everyone was complimenting Harry, so why did it feel like I needed to defend him?

"Thanks for that, wife," Harry whispered with a smile, his breath close to my ear.

"Just doing my part, husband," I whispered back, a smile spreading across my face, too.

~

"They'll kill you with kindness." Ruby offered me a glass of wine as we stood off to the side of the living room. The rest of Harry's family were still chatting out in the backyard, with Grace cornering Mom about their upcoming gardening project.

"What do you mean?"

"I mean, you did the right thing. Defending Harry." Ruby smiled. "It used to be like that with Sean, too. They'd compliment him to death about his IT job. Like it was the most important thing in the world. Like it was the only thing he was good at."

Ruby sipped at her glass of wine. "It adds a lot of pressure. Growing up like that. I think Grace and Jonah mean well, but it can be extremely limiting."

"I don't think they mean to do it. They don't seem like the type," I said. "Plus, they're so nice to me and my mom.

You'd think they might be snobs since we're so clearly from a different world. But they've never even mentioned it once."

"They're not cruel people. They just don't realize how they come across sometimes."

"It gets to Harry. The way they are."

"Of course it does." Ruby gave me a sympathetic nod. "It would get to everyone. And with how much they expect from him…"

"They sounded so sure about him running the company." I shook my head in confusion. "Which is so weird. Why would they even talk about handing it over to Sean? Why threaten Harry with losing his job as CEO?"

"Because threats still work even when they're empty."

I frowned. "What do you mean?"

"Can you keep a secret?" Ruby lowered her voice. "I'm serious, Simone. You can't tell Harry."

"What are you trying to tell me, Ruby?"

"Jonah and Grace never thought Harry was going to find someone. As in, ever. And then you came along and changed everything. We're all so happy that Harry met you, Simone."

Ruby went quiet for a moment before she went on.

"But I suspect that Harry's parents were never going to fire Harry as CEO. Even if he never got married by his fortieth birthday. Like I said, I love Sean, but he would've been a disaster for *LA Now*."

"Oh." I was nearly stunned into silence.

"I don't know for sure," Ruby said. "It's just what I think. Sean never said anything about it either way."

"Well, if your suspicions are correct, I guess the threats worked, then. If the point was just for him to meet someone."

I tried to keep the pain off my face as I took a sip of my

wine. A storm was brewing inside of me, with too many emotions coming up at once. I was angry for Harry's sake, upset that his family would put him through all of that stress for nothing.

But I was sad, too.

Because if Ruby was right, whatever there was between Harry and me meant even less than I had imagined. We weren't even saving Harry's job as CEO.

Maybe we were just playing pretend for no reason at all.

"This was for the best. Trust me." Ruby giggled, then winked. "I don't think Harry would've ever married you this fast if he didn't think he might lose his job. Which is so stupid since he's so clearly in love with you."

Clearly in love with me.

Sure.

I wanted to roll my eyes but I knew better. I didn't want Ruby to think that anything was wrong with what she'd just said.

Even if it wasn't true.

"When do you think you two will have children?" Ruby's question caught me completely off guard.

"Children?"

"You know, the little humans that run around all day? The ones who are super cute but will also totally drain your bank account if you take them to the toy store?"

"They still have toy stores?" I joked, as I thought about the best way to answer Ruby's question. "And I don't know."

"You don't know? As in, you don't know if you two want children?"

"As in, we haven't had that conversation yet."

"Really?" Ruby hummed, her brows creasing with concern.

"Really. But it's not like we've been avoiding the conversation. It just never came up."

"Well, I guess that's okay. As long as neither one of you is super against having kids. If it happens, it happens, right?"

"Right."

Ruby moved closer to me, then close enough to lean her head against my shoulder.

"I'm happy you're part of the family now, Simone." She sighed. "You're the best thing to happen to Harry in a long, long time."

17

HARRY

Finally.

I was home.

Brunch with my family had gone about as well as to be expected, considering I was in a fake marriage.

It seemed like Simone and Eileen were fitting in just fine, though. Which was good news and bad news, all at once. Good because I had a feeling my family genuinely liked them.

Bad because sooner or later, Simone and I were going to announce our divorce and they were never going to see each other again.

Still, I was grateful for the cover. Or at least, the cover I thought we had.

Shit.

I thought back to my mom talking about hearing that rumor.

Was that whole thing a misdirect? Did she actually know what was going on with Simone and me?

Was she just dangling the truth right in my face?

"Just got Mom down for her afternoon nap," Simone

said as she walked into the living room. "I think she may have had one too many mimosas during brunch. She never passes out like that."

"Is it okay if she drinks mimosas? With her condition?"

Simone stopped in her tracks. "Are you seriously asking about my mom's health?"

"You think I don't care about your mom's health?"

"No, it's just—" Simone shook her head. "That's just not the kind of thing I think you'd spend your time thinking about. It's not work-related so I figured it wasn't a priority."

"I care about more than just work, Simone," I said as I stepped toward her. "For example, I also really care about how you think brunch went with my family."

"I think it went pretty great."

"You don't think they suspected anything?" I pressed. "Not even my mom? I feel like that rumor thing she pulled with your mom was her trying to hint at something sideways."

"I don't think so, no. If anything, they seemed pretty pumped about the whole thing."

"The only thing they seemed pumped about was me keeping the company." I scoffed. "Even though they were willing to rip it all away over nothing. It's like, make up your mind. Either you want me to be CEO or you don't."

"They always wanted you to be CEO, Harry."

"Could've fooled me."

Simone went silent for a moment, like there was something weighing on her mind. Suddenly, she spoke. "I think they're just excited for us, you know? Excited for you. They're happy that you found someone."

"Right. Because if I hadn't found someone, they would've taken away my life's work just because I didn't fall in love based on their made-up timeline."

"You should give them more credit than that."

"Why?"

"Because they're your family. And they love you," Simone replied. "Because even if they make mistakes sometimes, they really do just want what's best for you."

"You're defending them again?" I took a step away from Simone. "Huh. I really thought you were starting to have my back here."

"I do have your back, Harry." Simone took a step toward me, closing the distance between us. "I just think you should cut them some slack. They're not perfect, but they really are trying."

"I don't believe in giving out trophies just for trying."

"No one's talking about giving out trophies." Simone reached for my hand. "I just think you don't know how good you have it sometimes. You still have both your parents. You have Sean and Ruby. You have Maxon."

Simone looked away from me as she went on. "It was so hard for my mom and me after we lost Dad. It was like everything just fell apart, all at once. My mom had to get used to life without him. She had to get used to being in her wheelchair, too. Meanwhile, I was going through my own personal hell. My dad was my best friend and he was just... gone."

Simone brought her gaze back to mine. "I know you have complicated feelings about your family, Harry. But you have no idea how much you're going to regret pushing them away when they're gone. Everything might be messy and confusing now, but you're going to miss all of that when you can't see them again."

"Simone." It was all I could say as I wrapped my palm around hers. "I'm sorry. I didn't mean to come off as ungrateful. I know what you've been through. It's just—"

"Complicated?"

"Extremely." I chuckled, trying my best to lighten the mood. "Especially since it feels like I'm never going to be good enough. Like I'm never going to fit in. I've always felt so different than what they expected me to be, Simone. I don't know if there's a cure for that."

"Nothing about you needs to be cured, Harry O'Donnell."

I smiled down at her as she leaned closer to me.

Just as I leaned closer to her.

But instead of a kiss, she pulled away, moving her hand back to her side.

"So, what did you and Ruby talk about?" I mirrored her, moving my hands back, too. "I noticed you two hanging out in the corner of the room. Looks like you two are getting close."

"Oh. She just wanted to know when we're going to have kids."

"Kids?" My heart started to race behind my chest. "She asked about when we're having kids? Why would she even ask something like that? You didn't bring it up first, did you?"

"Relax. I told her that it'll happen when it happens."

"But it's not going to happen, right?" I pressed. "It's never going to happen, right, Simone? Because you can't have kids?"

"Are you suggesting that I lied to you about not being able to have kids?" Simone narrowed her eyes at me. "Because that would be a really fucked-up thing to accuse me of, Harry."

"I'm not accusing you of anything. I just wanted to make sure we're on the same page."

"Of course we're on the same page." She scoffed. "I know

that none of this is real, Harry. Calm down. The only reason I didn't tell Ruby about my medical stuff is because we're not really family and I didn't feel like involving her in my personal life. She didn't need to know that I can't have kids."

She looked sad for a moment after she spoke, and a spark of jealousy flew through my veins.

Was Simone sad about not being able to have kids?

Or about not actually being a part of my family?

I wondered if she was going to miss them more than she was going to miss me.

But why did I care if she missed me at all?

"It's good, though. That we can't have kids," I said. "We don't want to make any permanent mistakes during our temporary situation."

"Yeah, I think you've made yourself clear on that." Simone nodded, something still so sad about her. "All right. I'm going to go catch up on my emails. We'll talk later?"

"Yep. Talk later." I waved her off, and she walked out of the room.

Images of playing catch with Maxon began to play in my head. For a brief moment, I wondered what it would've been like to be a dad instead of an uncle, to have a Maxon of my own running around brunch.

I wondered what it would've been like to chase after the kids with Simone, wrangling them to get ready for brunch, teaching them to have manners in public—

No.

I couldn't waste my time thinking about things that were never going to happen. Especially things that I didn't want to happen.

I didn't want that with Simone. I didn't want that with anyone.

It was just a tempting fantasy and nothing more.

18

SIMONE

I avoided Harry for the rest of the afternoon.

There was something about our conversation earlier, the way he wanted to be *sure* that I really couldn't have kids. It made me feel like I was suddenly living under a microscope, like he was going to be watching my every move to make sure I hadn't been lying to him.

Ugh.

Why'd he have to be like that? I knew he was different from his family, but couldn't he at least be a little warmer? A little more inviting?

They had their problems, sure, but they'd never made me feel like I was somehow in the wrong just for existing.

But maybe I wasn't really upset with Harry.

Maybe I was just upset because my conversation with Ruby had reminded me of how much I'd wanted to be a mother, and how impossible it was. I hadn't expected it to still hurt me as much as it did, but not being able to have kids still stung me in ways I never saw coming.

But the subject of kids seemed to sting Harry, too.

Did he really not want children? Or was he just reluctant to bring more kids into his family?

Maybe he just didn't want his kids growing up and feeling like he did, like outsiders in their own home.

Or maybe he was so deeply allergic to commitment that kids represented the ultimate kind of failure. After all, parenthood was the biggest commitment anyone could make.

Whatever it was, it was weighing on me. I was also feeling a strange disappointment at the idea that whatever Harry and I shared was built on a foundation of lies, that there wasn't anything real between us.

Because it meant we couldn't ever have a real conversation about anything, either.

Not about how we were feeling. Or weren't feeling.

Not even about the sting.

~

After dinner, I settled into bed with a good book.

I'd managed to avoid any awkward dinner table conversation by simply ordering takeout. My mom seemed grateful for the crab Rangoon while I was happy enough with black pepper chicken. I didn't see what Harry had ordered, mostly because I'd already headed back to my room with my dinner before he had a chance to say anything to me.

I still wasn't in the mood to speak to him.

Which is why it was so frustrating that I could hear him knocking on my bedroom door right now.

"Simone?" Harry asked as he stepped into the room. "You still awake?"

"What happens if I say no?"

"I feel like a jerk for waking you up." Harry smirked. "But I had a feeling you'd still be up. I saw the light on underneath your door."

I held up my book. "Good catch. I was going to read for a bit before bed."

"Cool. Reading sounds fun." It was all Harry said as he stared at me, his eyes fixed on mine.

A few seconds passed before he took a step toward my bed. And then another.

And another.

He didn't stop until he was inches away from my mattress, his gaze still locked on mine. The look in his eye was familiar, the same way he'd look at me in the middle of the night when moonlight was spilling across my naked frame.

The same way he'd look at me when he was moving inside of me, his hips pressed against mine.

"Harry? Did you need something?" I asked as I looked up at him.

I didn't move a muscle, not inviting him into my bed but not discouraging it, either. I was still annoyed with him, but I couldn't pretend that I didn't want him.

All he had to do was ask, and I would've given him every inch of me.

He hesitated, still wordless as he watched me.

I reached for him then, gently pulling him toward the bed. His knee sank into the mattress, his face inches away from mine.

Our lips gently brushed against each other's, almost like a kiss but not quite.

But then he moved away from me.

Away from my bed. Away from my room.

Without a word, Harry headed back out into the hall, the scent of his cologne the only thing he left behind.

What the hell was that?

I was used to Harry climbing into my bed for the night. I wasn't used to him making a half-hearted attempt at it before leaving my room without saying anything.

It was like he'd changed his mind in a matter of seconds.

Maybe he wanted me to follow him back to his room? Maybe it was some kind of test?

"Whatever," I muttered before flopping down against my mattress. "I don't have time for those kinds of mind games."

I literally didn't have time. I needed to get my rest, especially since I was taking my mom to an appointment in the morning. I closed my eyes and tried to force myself to go to sleep.

But it wasn't working.

Great.

I reached for my phone, intent on scrolling through social media until I got sleepy from reading all the posts and headlines. Just as I was on the fifteenth meme post about a cute cat begging for food it didn't need, I felt my phone begin to shake with an incoming call.

"Taylor?" I answered the phone, pulling it close to my ear. "You're not asleep yet?"

"Ew. What? Why would I be asleep?" Taylor chuckled. "You're the one on married people time. Not me. I'm still free as a bird, which means I can stay up as long as I want."

"I'm not on married people time, either, Taylor." I frowned.

"Uh, why do you sound sad about that?"

"I sound sad?"

"Yeah. You sound really disappointed." Taylor hummed. "Did something happen with you and Harry?"

"Nothing happened. Which might be the problem."

"What do you mean?"

"Remember how you said that you think we should just let what happens, happen?" I sighed. "I'm worried that something is happening... but I'm the only one it's happening to."

"Are you trying to be vague on purpose? What are you talking about, babe?"

"I think I like Harry. As in, actually like him."

"Really?" Taylor gasped. "Oh my God! Simone!"

"You can calm down. I'm pretty sure he doesn't feel the same."

"What makes you say that?"

"Maybe because he's still so committed to this fake marriage thing? It feels like whenever we get close to something real, it freaks him out."

"You want me to tell you something that will either make you feel a lot better or a whole lot worse?"

"No?"

"You want to hear this. Trust me," Taylor said. "So, everyone at work already knew about the weird arrangement Harry had with his family, the whole needing to be married by his fortieth birthday thing."

"And?"

"And we've all seen the honeymoon pics on social media. No one in the office can tell if you two got married just to fulfill an obligation to his family or if it's some kind of Cinderella story."

"How is that good news?"

"It's good news because it means that no one can tell if it's real or fake. Looking from the outside, it seems like it's real between you two. Which makes me wonder if you're not the only one starting to feel something real."

"I just wish I knew if he was feeling it, too." I groaned. "And I'm starting to feel like an idiot for jumping into this whole thing, anyway. It would be so much easier if we were just dating like normal people."

"If you were dating like normal people, you wouldn't be together." Taylor reminded me. "Besides, it's possible that you're just inhaling too many of Harry's pheromones. You two are around each other too much. Maybe you don't even like him. You just like the way he smells."

"Sounds primal."

"I just don't want you to forget that you used to think Harry was a total dick." She laughed. "Seriously. If this doesn't work out, I don't want you moping around. It's not like it was love at first sight or something."

"You're right. I'll make sure to keep my moping to a minimum." I laughed now, too. "Thanks for the reminder, Taylor."

"Anytime, babe." Taylor chuckled again. "Now, get some sleep, okay? Don't stay up all night being worried over some guy."

"Don't worry about me. I'm headed off to dreamland now. Night, Taylor."

"Night, babe!"

I ended the phone call with a smile on my face, even as I tossed and turned throughout the rest of the night. I still couldn't get to sleep, and worse, I was breaking my promise to Taylor.

Because I was definitely staying up all night worried over some guy.

19

HARRY

I didn't know why I went to Simone's room last night.

It was almost like a compulsion, like I knew that was where I was supposed to be. I couldn't even say that it was about sex, although as soon as I saw her, every part of me wanted her.

But it was more than sex.

What I wanted most of all was to be *with* her, cuddled up against her, feeling her soft skin and breathing in her scent.

Shit.

Sliding into her bed was starting to feel way too natural to me.

What's going on with me lately?

The whole thing had been embarrassing, especially since I'd mostly just stood there staring at her like an idiot. The fact that I almost kissed her made things even worse, like I was flip-flopping in real time.

"Good morning!" Simone beamed as she greeted me in the kitchen. "Did you sleep well last night?"

"I slept pretty good, yeah," I lied. I didn't feel like

explaining to her that I'd struggled to get to sleep last night after my strange visit to her bedroom. "How about you?"

"I slept pretty good, too." She beamed again. "I'm kind of excited, actually, about Mom's doctor's appointment. She's never had hope like this before, with the potential surgery. I think it could be really good if everything works out."

"Did you want me to come with you?"

"Nope. I got it." She nodded. "It's not my first rodeo with doctors. Oh, you remembered to take me off the schedule for this morning, right?"

Nope. "Yeah, don't worry about it."

I was too busy tossing and turning last night to even take a glance at the schedule for today. Thankfully, I knew that even if I wasn't exactly on top of it, Paul would still have my back.

Thank God for Paul.

"Great! I'll see you later?" Simone hastily poured herself a cup of coffee. "Maybe tonight?"

"Yep, see you tonight." I barely had a chance to get the words out before Simone was out of the room.

Wait.

Was she running away from me? From how happy she seemed, it felt like she was barely thinking about what happened between us last night. But with how short our conversation was just now, I was starting to get the feeling that she didn't appreciate how things had ended in her bedroom.

Shit.

I needed to do something to make things right, didn't I?

"Are you okay, sir?" Paul placed a stack of documents on my desk. "You've been pretty quiet all morning."

I'd been closed off in my office ever since I stepped through the doors of *LA Now*. It was never hard for me to make myself busy, with all the interview requests, headline reviews, and article submissions I had to sort through on a daily basis.

Still, it felt like I was on autopilot. Like I was just going through the motions necessary to get me through the day.

Like I was just killing time until I had a chance to redeem myself with Simone.

"Just marriage stuff." I shrugged as I pulled the documents closer to me. "You know how it is."

"Uh, no. I don't." Paul chuckled. "You know I've never been married. Hell, I haven't even been engaged."

"Right. Well." I looked up at Paul. "It's complicated."

"Complicated how?"

"I think I fucked up, that's how. And I don't know how to unfuck the situation."

"How'd you fuck up?"

"That's irrelevant."

"Got it. So, you want me to help you without actually giving me any information." Paul nodded. "Can you at least give me a hint about how you fucked up? Lack of empathy? Putting pressure on her about something she wasn't ready for?"

"I... failed to communicate how I felt about something in the moment."

"About something? Or about her?"

"I don't know," I admitted. "I don't know what I was thinking. Or what I was trying to say."

"And you think she might be upset with you about it?"

"I don't think she's upset, Paul. I *know* she is."

"Huh." Paul rested a fist beneath his chin. "Is she close with her mom? She lives with you two now, right?"

"Yeah, but I don't see how that matters—"

"You should do something nice for her mom."

"What?" I shook my head in confusion. "How is doing something nice for her mom going to make things right between Simone and me?"

"Because it's going to catch her off guard. You do something nice for Simone? Maybe get her some flowers? Who cares?" Paul scoffed. "But you do something nice for her mom? She'll probably forgive whatever fucked-up thing you did just like that. It's an unexpected kindness. It's hard to ignore something like that."

"That's actually a genius idea."

"Don't be so surprised." Paul laughed. "There's a reason you hired me to be your right-hand man, sir."

Paul snapped his fingers before he spoke again. "What about the house? Did you already make it accessible for her mom's wheelchair?"

"Yep. Already taken care of." A thought suddenly popped into my head. "But there's still something else I could do for her. Something I think she'd really appreciate."

"What are you thinking, boss?"

"I think I'm going to build a wheelchair accessible greenhouse in my backyard." I grinned. "Eileen said she loves gardening but it's harder for her nowadays, after the accident. What if I could make it easy for her again?"

"Holy shit." Paul's eyes went wide. "That's the kind of thing that would make a woman want to marry you."

Paul held up a finger. "Wait. Uh, sir?"

"Yeah, Paul?"

"Is this real?" Paul asked, his voice low. "I kind of thought you just wanted to smooth things over with Simone since you two are living together. But it's starting to feel like you're trying to make things right with your actual wife?"

"Simone is my actual wife, Paul." I nodded toward my office door with a grin. "Now, clear the rest of your schedule for the day. I'm going to need you to find out who can put together a greenhouse this evening."

20

SIMONE

"It's going to be okay, Mom. You're going to be okay."

I was sitting next to my mother in the doctor's office and nervously tapping my foot. We'd only signed into the office five minutes ago, but it felt like things were taking forever.

My mom, on the other hand, didn't seem to share my nervous energy. "Relax, Simi. Everything's going to be fine."

"That's what I just said, Mom. Everything's going to be okay."

"Yes, but you didn't mean it." She lightly chuckled before taking my hand in her own. "Don't worry. The worst thing they can say is no. Nothing else is going to change."

"I think getting a 'no' is still pretty bad, all on its own."

"You worry too much."

"Or maybe you don't worry enough?"

My mom waved away my concern before she turned her attention toward the office door. I watched the door, too, impatiently waiting for the doctor to step into the room.

When she did, I nearly jumped out of my seat as I ran over to greet her.

"Dr. Jimenez?" I held out my hand for her to shake. "You're Dr. Jimenez, right?"

"That's right." She beamed back at me as she shook my hand. "And you must be Simone and Eileen."

"Thank you so much for meeting with us today," my mom said from across the room. "I'm sure you're a very busy woman."

"Meeting with people is my job." Dr. Jimenez motioned for me to have a seat next to my mom. "And I'm always happy to do it. Especially when I have good news."

"Good news?" I stood by my mother's wheelchair, filled with way too much anxious energy to sit down.

"Yes." Dr. Jimenez pulled a manila folder out from underneath her arm. "Eileen, we just got your scans back from the lab. It looks like you're an excellent candidate for the spinal fusion surgery."

"Really?" Mom's eyes started to water. "Oh my God. I was hopeful, but I wasn't sure. I never thought this day would come."

Yes.

Yes! Yes! Yes!

My eyes started to water, too, as the good news sank in. I turned toward my mother, bending down to take her into my arms.

Except when I reached for her, my arms suddenly felt like two wet noodles hanging from my shoulders.

I blinked, and for a couple of seconds, my world went dark.

"Simi? Simi!" I heard my mom's voice as I collapsed into the chair beside her.

Ugh.

I was so dizzy that the room was spinning. I brought a

hand to the side of my head, hoping that somehow, I'd be able to bring everything back into focus.

"Simone? Are you feeling all right?" Dr. Jimenez asked as she walked up to me.

"Yeah. I'm fine."

"Well, you just fainted," she said. "Hearing good news can sometimes have that effect on people, but I need to make sure you're okay. Have you been getting enough sleep?"

"Honestly? No. I've been struggling a little in the sleep department."

"Hmm." She slightly tilted her head. "Are you on birth control right now? When was the last time you had your period?"

"Funny."

"Why is that funny?"

"Because it sounds like you're trying to figure out if I'm pregnant, but I *can't* get pregnant, Dr. Jimenez. I have severe endometriosis that left me infertile."

"Endometriosis doesn't necessarily mean you can never get pregnant, Simone. It makes things harder, sure. But it's usually not impossible." She kept her focus on me as she calmly asked again, "When was your last period, Simone?"

"Actually, I think I might be late," I quietly admitted. "But with the whole lack of sleep thing, I probably just screwed up my cycle."

"You should take a pregnancy test. If we offered tests here, I'd certainly offer you one right now."

"Eh. I think a pregnancy test would just be a waste of money."

"There's no harm in checking. If you're right, you're right," she replied. "But if I'm right, I think it's best to know as far in advance as you can."

"Sure thing," I finally agreed with a nod. "I'll take a test, then. Just to be on the safe side."

And so you'll get off my back about it.

I knew that Dr. Jimenez meant well, but it was painful to have her suggest I get a pregnancy test when I knew better. I knew that my chances of pregnancy were astronomically small. Why did she have to remind me of that today?

And why did it still hurt so much?

"As for you, Eileen." Dr. Jimenez turned toward my mom. "We'll need to run a few more tests, just to make sure everything's in order. You can stop by the nurse's desk on your way out and they'll help you set up the appointments you'll need for blood work."

"Sounds good to me, Doctor." My mom smiled wide. "Thank you. Thank you so much."

"Of course." Dr. Jimenez smiled back. "Do you have any questions for me now?"

Mom began to ask her some questions about the surgery, and I tried my best to listen to the doctor's responses.

But inside, I was a mess.

~

"Do you think she's right, Simi? Do you think you're pregnant?"

The cab ride home from the doctor's office had been mostly silent, except for the occasional song on the radio or a honking horn. I'd been lost in thought as I imagined my mom getting her mobility back and being in less pain.

"Do I think I'm pregnant?" I playfully scoffed. "I don't

know, Mom. That's like asking me if I think the moon is made out of cheese."

"You really don't think there's a chance?"

"No. I don't," I said. "After all those doctors I saw with Jace? All those tests and ultrasounds? Every one of those doctors told us the same thing, Mom. Getting pregnant naturally just isn't in the cards for me."

"Doctors can be wrong, Simi." My mom sighed. "They were wrong about me, weren't they? They didn't think there was anything that anyone could ever do for me. And here we are, talking with Dr. Jimenez about surgery."

"That's different, Mom. That's about there being advances in technology, you know? In my case, there'd have to be some kind of technological advance in my *womb*. And unless there's a little robot inside of me that I don't know about, I don't think that's happening anytime soon."

"You really don't think there's a chance?" Her voice was low. "As in, you and Harry haven't...?"

"Mom!"

"Listen to me, Simi." She leaned closer to me, like she was telling me a secret. "I don't need to know any of the details about you and Harry. And technically, you're a married woman so you're free to do what you want. I just want to make sure you're being realistic about things."

"Okay. Yes. There's a chance," I murmured back. "But it's such a small chance that it doesn't matter."

"I knew it." My mom bit into a smile as she moved away from me.

"You knew what?"

"That you liked him."

"You're not upset about it?" I was puzzled by her response. "I thought you wanted me to find true love or have some kind of epic romance."

"You think I don't have eyes?"

"Mom, what are you—"

"No one knows they're in the middle of an epic romance until they're on the other side of it, Simone." She gently patted my hand. "You and Harry have some potential. I wouldn't count him out just yet."

"Harry doesn't feel that way about me, Mom."

"And you're sure about that?"

"I'm sure that it doesn't matter, even if he does. I'm sure that this is just a business arrangement for him and once it's over, I'll go back to being one of his employees like nothing ever happened."

"I guess we'll just have to wait and see." It was the last thing she said before she looked out her window, her mind already somewhere else.

I couldn't know for sure, but I had a feeling that she was back in Paris, taking a stranger up on his offer to show her the way to the Eiffel Tower.

～

After I dropped my mom off back at the guesthouse at Harry's place, I added a stop to the cab ride.

The pharmacy.

It didn't take long for me to grab a pregnancy test and hop back in the cab. I held the plastic bag close to my chest, like I was transporting national secrets.

I didn't know why it felt like such a big deal to me, since I pretty much knew what the answer was going to be: *Not Pregnant.*

I comforted myself with the thought as I stepped into my bathroom back at Harry's home. I did the usual song and dance, peeing on the stick and trying my best to pretend like I didn't care about the results.

Because I didn't care. Because I *couldn't* care.

Because being invested in the results was historically a very good way to end up with a broken heart.

I pushed the memories away as I waited for the results to pop up on the screen. Memories of Jace trying to comfort me after another negative result. Memories of trying to hold back the tears. Memories of feeling so hopeless, so helpless—

No.

I couldn't let myself spiral like that. This was different, wasn't it? This time, I *wanted* the test to be negative.

I wanted the test to give me its usual answer. I wanted things to be the same as they always were—

"Oh my God."

My hands shook as I held the test, an unfamiliar reading appearing across the screen.

Pregnant.

"Pregnant?" I mouthed the word, my body feeling almost too heavy to stand. "I'm pregnant?"

I sank down against the side of the bathtub, needing something to lean on for support.

"How?" I turned the test over in my hand, like it was a sacred artifact from a museum. "How is that even possible?"

I needed to tell Taylor. I needed to tell my mom.

Crap.

I needed to tell my OB/GYN!

I reached for my phone, hastily dialing my gynecologist's number, now desperate for an appointment.

21

HARRY

"Is there a reason we're not having dinner out on the patio on such a lovely night?" Simone asked as she rolled Eileen into the dining room. "And is there a reason we had to use the side entrance to get in the main house?"

It turned out that getting the bare bones of a greenhouse built in a day wasn't impossible, it was just very, very expensive. It also didn't help that the greenhouse had to be built as far away as possible from Eileen's guesthouse, with added instructions for the builders to be as quiet as mice.

Of course, quiet as mice involved me adding a few thousand dollars onto their invoice.

Still, I was pleased with the fruit of Paul's idea. I was so pleased that I could hardly contain my excitement–which was a problem since Simone and Eileen were in a sour kind of mood.

Shit.

Did they get bad news about Eileen's surgery?

"Is everything all right?" I asked. "How did the appointment go?"

"The appointment went great." Eileen immediately brightened. "I'm a good candidate for the surgery. They just need to run a few more tests."

That same brightness then faded away as she went on. "I think it's just a lot to handle. I've never had a chance like this before. But it's not a miracle cure. It's possible that they perform the surgery and nothing changes for me. Or they somehow make things worse."

"We made the mistake of looking up the success rates for something like this," Simone added. "I think maybe we got ahead of ourselves when we got the good news from the doctor."

"I don't know. Kind of sounds like we should celebrate to me." I grinned. "Good news is still good news. How about we open a bottle of champagne?"

"No!" Simone quickly shook her head. "No champagne."

"Simi's right. I'm not sure I'm in the mood for champagne, either." Eileen sighed. "I would like to eat dinner now, though."

"Sure," I said, heading to the door. "I'm hungry, too."

"Need any help serving?" Simone asked.

"Nah, I've got it." I waved her off.

In the kitchen, I plated the dinner I'd had catered by a professional chef. Eileen and Simone quietly spoke to each other at the dinner table, their tone somber and serious. Sometimes, I'd look over and see Simone or Eileen smiling, but it seemed short-lived.

Dammit.

I felt like a total idiot. Here I was, so ready to spring the greenhouse news on Simone and Eileen. But for all they knew, Eileen was going to be in even worse shape than before.

There was a chance she wouldn't have even been able to appreciate the greenhouse.

"Dinner's served," I said as I set plates down in front of Eileen, Simone, and then myself. As I took my seat, I looked over at Eileen. "And Eileen?"

"Yes, Harry?"

"I hope the surgery goes well for you. I hope it gives you back at least some of what you lost. And I hope that somehow it helps you find new parts of yourself, too."

"Thank you, Harry. That's so sweet of you." Eileen smiled.

"Yeah, Harry. That was really sweet." Simone smiled at me, too. "And you can tell whoever made this dinner that it smells out of this world."

Dinner went by without much conversation, as mother and daughter exchanged glances only they understood. It was like watching them speak in a secret language, even though I knew why they didn't want to let me in right now.

They were scared, panicked about the surgery. They were excited about it, too.

It had to be a confusing mix of emotions, and I had no interest in pressuring them to let me in as they worked through everything they felt.

Once dinner was over, Simone escorted Eileen back to the guesthouse, using the side door as I requested. When Simone finished putting her mother to bed, she returned to the house, bringing the dishes from the dining room table to the sink.

"Sorry about dinner being a little weird," she started. "This surgery thing with my mom is a little heavier than I think either of us realized. It kind of just hit us all at once."

"That's okay. I can only imagine how you two are feeling right now."

"You never answered my question, by the way."

"What question?"

"Why are you making us use the side entrance?" She turned the hot water on in the sink. "Did we lose our access privileges to the other doors?"

"Yep. That's it." I laughed. "You and your mom have been way too disrespectful toward the other doors in this home. This is the only way you're ever going to learn your lesson."

"I knew it!" Simone laughed now, too. "This has been your game plan all along. Have us move in with you so you can get us to play these twisted games!"

"Guilty as charged." I playfully nudged her in the shoulder. "Seriously, though. It's a surprise."

"Ooh, that sounds fun. What's the surprise?"

"If I tell you, that's going to ruin the whole thing."

"Boo!" Simone flicked a few soap bubbles my way before she broke into another laugh. "Fine, then, Harry. Keep your secrets."

I couldn't help but stare at her, taking in every second of her happiness and joy. Simone was always beautiful, but she was especially beautiful in moments like these, when she completely let her guard down.

"What's going on?" Simone stared back at me. "What is it? Is there something on my face?"

"Oh, uh, no." I stumbled over my words. "I just, uh, wanted to tell you that if you needed to take a leave of absence from work to deal with the surgery with your mom, I'd be okay with that."

"Really?"

"Yep. And you could come back whenever you're ready. I'll just hold your job for you."

"Thanks. I'll probably take you up on that." Simone

sighed. "I have a feeling it's going to be a bit intense for a while."

She gripped the counter suddenly as she swayed a little by the sink.

"Hey. Are you feeling okay?" I wrapped an arm around her waist, keeping her in place.

"Yeah. I'm fine. Just a little tired, I think."

"Sounds like you should go to bed, then."

"I think I'll take you up on that, too." Simone set the clean plate down beside the sink. "I'll see you in the morning?"

"See you in the morning."

I let her out of my grasp, even though I didn't want to. I wanted to follow behind her as she went to bed. I wanted to make sure she was truly okay and keep a watchful eye over her until she fell fast asleep.

I wanted to hold her close to me all through the night.

Fuck.

This was bad. This was really, really bad.

It was one thing to crave Simone physically, but wanting to comfort her? Wanting to share a bed with her just for the sake of it?

If I didn't get a grip soon, I was going to reach a point of no return.

Besides, it wasn't like I'd ever been a cuddler, anyway. So, why the hell was I trying to start now?

I forced myself to stay by the sink, despite everything inside of me wanting to go knock on her door.

She's tired. She wouldn't want to see you, anyway.

I repeated the words in my head. But the more I heard them, the more I felt I was lying to myself.

Like I was trying to convince myself of something that just wasn't true.

22

SIMONE

How was I going to tell Harry?

I paced up and down my bedroom the next morning, my mind racing with a million thoughts a minute.

He didn't want kids. He'd told me that about a dozen times over.

What would be the point of even telling him of my pregnancy? So he could say he wasn't interested in being a dad? That I'd made an awful mistake, and he didn't want any part of it?

But that was just it. I didn't feel like I'd made a mistake.

The life possibly growing inside of me didn't feel like a *mistake*.

And I didn't want to pretend for even a second I regretted it.

Which meant that if I really was pregnant, I'd have to raise the baby all by myself. Even if it was going to be difficult managing my mother's health at the same time, I knew it was the only way.

I took a deep breath as I reached into my closet, picking

out my clothes for the day. I had a long day ahead of me, filled with lab appointments for my mom. I'd already sent an email to the office requesting leave from my job so I could be with her, even though the thought of it made me feel queasier than I already did.

I was grateful to Harry for giving me the option to take leave, but I couldn't help but wonder what the people at work were going to say. It looked like I was getting special treatment for being Harry's wife, and I was.

Special treatment for a special woman.

Except Harry didn't seem to think that I was all that special.

Whatever.

I pushed those thoughts away as I finished getting ready for the day.

And soon, I was headed out the door.

"You don't have to wait here with me, Simi," my mom said as she held out her arm for the lab tech to draw blood. We were sitting in yet another medical office.

"Of course I'm going to stay here with you, Mom. You really think I'm going to let you go through this alone?"

"I've been through this before, dear." She patted me on the shoulder. "You should go. This part is so boring, anyway."

"Only if you're sure."

"I'm sure." She nodded. "Maybe you could run a few errands and come back for me later? Maybe grab me a bag of chips while you're out?"

"Ah. That's your real game, isn't it?" I smirked. "If you

wanted me to grab you a snack, Mom, that's all you had to say."

She laughed.

I playfully rolled my eyes as I stood up from my seat. "I'll be back, okay? With your snack. Promise. And if you need anything in the meantime, just shoot me a text."

I looked over at the nurse before I spoke again. "Take good care of her, yeah? And don't be afraid to call me about anything."

"Of course, ma'am. We'll take good care of her while you're gone."

∼

"Simone?" Dr. Carlson looked almost surprised to see me, even though I knew I had to be on her schedule. I'd requested an appointment at the very last minute, and thankfully, her nurses had been able to fit me in. "What brings you in today?"

Dr. Carlson had been my gynecologist for years, including when I was desperately trying to get pregnant with Jace. I briefly wondered if she was just as traumatized by everything as I was–all the heartbreak, all the false hope.

"Pregnancy test." I held up my arm, showing her where a nurse had just placed a cotton ball and a Band-Aid after drawing blood. "I wanted to do it the old-fashioned way, just to be sure."

"I'm not sure if most people would consider a blood test old-fashioned." Dr. Carlson chuckled. "Besides, home pregnancy tests are quite accurate these days."

"But there's always room for error, isn't there?"

"Sure, yes. There's always room for error," she agreed. "But it's a fairly small margin."

The Wedding Hoax

She paused as she looked me over, like she was trying to read my mind. "Has something changed recently, Simone?"

"I took a pregnancy test."

"And?"

"It said that I was pregnant," I went on. "But that didn't make any sense, so I wanted to get a second opinion."

"It didn't make any sense? Meaning you haven't been sexually active lately or—"

"Oh. No. I've been sexually active. It's just that we both know that I'm infertile. So, I just wanted to make sure there wasn't something else going on."

"I never said that you were infertile, Simone." Dr. Carlson's face turned serious. "There was always a chance of natural pregnancy, even if it was low. There might a ten percent chance of conceiving naturally, but that's a lot higher than zero."

"It didn't feel a lot higher than zero." I weakly laughed, even as painful memories threatened to play in the back of my mind. "It didn't feel like there was really any hope at all."

"Your odds went even higher if you considered IVF." Dr. Carlson held up my chart, seemingly for emphasis. "Your chances of conceiving went up to fifteen to twenty percent. I always made sure to tell you and Jace that IVF was another option—"

"It wasn't high enough."

"What?"

"The odds weren't high enough for him," I murmured. "He didn't think it was worth shelling out thousands of dollars for anything less than fifty percent. Maybe even seventy-five."

"And is he still your primary partner?"

"No. Jace and I broke up a while back."

"Just between you and me... good." Dr. Carlson cleared

her throat. "I know I'm not supposed to get involved in the personal lives of my patients, but I was always so worried about you with him, Simone. There was always so much pressure on you when you were here, like you were trying to pass some kind of test. It honestly broke my heart."

"That's how it felt. Like I was failing a test."

"You weren't. This was never a test, Simone." Dr. Carlson placed my chart underneath her arm. "Even now, if this pregnancy fails for any reason—"

"You think it's going to fail?" There was suddenly a lump in my throat.

"I'm not going to sugarcoat this. If you are indeed pregnant, then this would be a high-risk pregnancy. Not to mention that there could be adhesions in your womb that could make carrying the baby even more difficult."

"Got it. I could be pregnant and everything could still go wrong."

Dr. Carlson placed a soft hand on my shoulder. "Let's take it one day at a time, okay? The lab will be in touch with you if your blood work comes back positive for pregnancy. And we can go from there."

I nodded in agreement, even as the lump in my throat made its way down to my stomach.

I was terrified that I was pregnant. And terrified that I wasn't.

The worst part was that I couldn't tell anyone yet. I couldn't tell Taylor because I didn't want to get her hopes up. She knew how much I wanted a baby, and I wasn't ready to hear the sadness in her voice if I had to tell her that the pregnancy didn't quite take.

I couldn't tell my mom, either, not with all her current tests and surgery preparations. She needed to be focused on her own health stuff. It wasn't fair to burden her by bringing her back into my pregnancy chaos.

She'd been through enough already with Jace and me.

But what hurt the most was that I couldn't even tell Harry. I already knew that he'd want nothing to do with this baby. Even if I managed a healthy pregnancy, it was going to mean nothing to him.

There was a chance I was finally going to pass the pregnancy test, and the person I'd be passing with couldn't care less.

A familiar sting began to radiate pain through my skin as I left Dr. Carlson's office and went in search of a vending machine, grabbing my mom a snack before I went back to the lab.

~

"You're pregnant, Simone."

"What?" I blinked slowly, confused by Dr. Carlson's words. "I'm sorry. I think I heard you wrong?"

It'd been a day since I'd been at Dr. Carlson's office. In the meantime, I'd been keeping myself busy with anxious cleaning. I'd gotten to the stage when I reorganized everything inside my dresser drawers, when I saw Dr. Carlson's number lighting up my phone.

"I think you heard me just fine, Simone." Her tone was lined with a smile. "You're pregnant. Congratulations."

"Oh my God!" I unintentionally screamed into the phone. "Oh my God! It's happening! It's really happening!"

"Yes, it really is." Dr. Carlson's voice was calm. "I'd like to book you for your first prenatal appointment. You could look at your calendar and get back to me or—"

"Put me down for the first one you have available. I'll be there." I squealed again before I added, "Thank you so much, Dr. Carlson! Thank you!"

I hastily ended the call before I dialed Taylor's number.

"Taylor! Meet me at the coffee shop ASAP."

"Simone, it's 10:00 a.m.," Taylor groaned. "Are you asking me to take an early lunch for this?"

"You won't regret it. Trust me." I forced myself to keep my next squeal inside. "Bye! I'll see you there!"

Around fifteen minutes later, Taylor and I were sitting at a table in the corner of the coffee shop. Taylor looked put together, as always, even though she seemed a little more tired than usual.

"I'm trying a new sleep routine," she offered, like she was able to read my mind. "There's this thing about trying to match your sleep cycle to your natural rhythm."

"And? Is it working?"

"According to my natural rhythm, I'm supposed to sleep in four-hour batches." Taylor frowned. "And yet, for some mysterious reason, it feels like I'm tired all the time."

"Probably because no one's supposed to sleep in four-hour batches?"

"I'm going to give it a few more days before calling it quits." She took a sip of her coffee. "I'm either going to prove everyone wrong, or I'm going to pass out in the middle of a meeting."

"I feel like Harry wouldn't appreciate that."

"Well, if he tries to fire me, I'll just remind him that I'm the reason he met his wife."

"Solid plan." I smirked.

"Anyway, what's up?" Taylor slightly shifted in her seat. "What was the big emergency you wanted me to come down here for?"

"Oh, nothing." I casually shrugged. "Just that I'm pregnant."

Taylor's eyes went wide. "Okay, either this is a hallucination caused by my sleep deprivation, or you just told me you're pregnant."

"It's the latter. I'm pregnant." I smiled wide. "I'm really pregnant, Taylor."

Taylor held up a hand. "Before I react, I need to know. Are we happy about this? Are we feeling weird about this?"

Her mouth suddenly fell open. "Wait. Is it Harry's? Was this on purpose? Are you trying to make sure your baby's some kind of heir?"

"I'm happy about this. Really happy." I beamed. "And yes, it's Harry's. But it wasn't on purpose. In fact, he has no idea."

"But you're going to tell him, right?"

"Yes, I will. Eventually, when the time is right. But there's a part of me that wonders if I even should tell him at all. I already know that he doesn't want kids, Taylor. And when I tell him the news, he might think I planned it. That I'm some kind of evil mastermind who's after his money or something."

"You really think he'd accuse you of something like that?"

"He might." I looked down at the table. "He might not want anything to do with me after he finds out."

Taylor reached a hand across the table. "Hey. Simone. Look at me."

I offered her my hand in return, right before she spoke again. "Even if Harry isn't going to be there for you, I'm going to be there. I'm with you every step of the way, babe."

"I know, Taylor." I smiled again. "Thank you for that."

"Duh. Anytime."

23

HARRY

Five days.

It'd been five days since Simone and I had a full-length conversation. Everything between us lately seemed to be exchanging greetings before I left for work or short chitchat if we happened to bump into each other around the house.

But there hadn't been anything more than that.

It felt like I'd been *reduced* somehow, like I'd gone from being her temporary husband to just another coworker.

Maybe even less than a coworker.

Hell, maybe I was just some guy she *knew from work*.

"Uh, sir? Are you doing okay?" Paul was seated beside me in the conference room. "You seem a little distracted."

"I'm good," I lied. "I was just reviewing the numbers again in my head."

"They're good numbers. Strong. I think everyone's going to be pretty happy."

"Let's hope so. I'm not really in the mood for massive layoffs."

"Whoa. Did someone say something about massive

layoffs?" Paul leaned in close, his tone filled with concern. "Because I kind of thought this was more about showing off the next issue of the magazine—"

"No. Sorry." I let out a tired sigh. "That was just my fucked-up attempt at being funny."

"Right. Good one." Paul shook his head as he looked down at the folder in his hands. There was a proposed layout for the next big issue of LA Now, the pages all set together and glossy.

I'd been working my ass off to get the next issue to the printers, and since early numbers showed that copies would be flying off the shelves, I wanted to do a victory lap in front of our advertisers and digital marketing team. It was half sales pitch and half informative meeting, giving me a chance to show off our numbers while also hopefully inspiring them to recruit more businesses to work with us.

It was how LA Now had stayed alive all this time.

I was a master at building up my own hype.

I smiled to myself, proud of the legacy I'd built for my family's company. But just as fast as my smile had spread across my face, it faded away.

Simone.

Five days.

She was still in the back of my head, even when I wasn't thinking about her.

How could she go five days without having a real conversation with me?

"You're sure you're okay, boss? Because you look like you're somewhere else right now." Paul was still looking at the printed copy of the magazine, but it felt like he was reading my mind. "It might be a good idea to reschedule if there's something else going on—"

"I'm good. Let's do this." I put my game face on before I

reached for the remote for the oversized TV screen in the center of the conference room.

A few seconds later, I started the virtual meeting, with faces joining in from around the world.

I'd have to figure out things with Simone later.

~

"Dinner was really good tonight."

I started the conversation just as I grabbed for Simone's plate. We'd ordered in, trying out a new Thai place that'd just opened up last month. Eileen had gone to bed a little earlier than usual, excusing herself from the table after she finished.

"Yeah. It was excellent, wasn't it?" Simone smiled. "Thanks for giving it a chance."

"Oh, I'm always willing to give two things a chance: peace and noodles."

"Funny," Simone said without the barest hint of a laugh. "Did you need help with the dishes? Or do you mind if I head up to bed, too?"

"You're going to bed already?"

"Unless you wanted me to help with the dishes," she reminded me. "Or if you wanted to talk to me about something else?"

Yeah, Simone, I do want to talk to you about something else. Why the hell are you treating me like this?

I tried to bury my frustration deep in my chest as I asked, "Are you okay?"

"Yeah. I'm fine. Why?"

"Nothing." I shrugged, pretending like everything was fine. "It's nothing. We just haven't really had a chance to catch up in a while since I've been so busy at work."

"Right. The next issue of *LA Now*. I think Taylor mentioned something about that. She's been pulling all-nighters trying to chase down permission rights for this big interview."

"And that's why Taylor's one of the best." I chuckled. "She doesn't stop until she gets what she wants."

"I guess you two have that in common." Simone smiled before she stood up from the table. "All right, then. I'll see you in the morning?"

"Yep. I'll see you in the morning. Good night—" I started and stopped myself, as I watched Simone leave the room before I even had a chance to finish what I was saying.

I couldn't do this anymore.

I couldn't pretend like everything was okay. I couldn't keep our conversations so casual and so light.

I missed Simone. I missed the real her. I missed our deep talks, the way she'd give me shit, the way she always had something to say.

It was obvious that she was keeping me at arm's length, and I needed to know why.

Was she getting sick of me? Had she hated me the whole time?

I paused outside of her bedroom as another thought slowly crept across my mind.

What if she's falling for me?

It would've explained all her recent behavior, how she was avoiding me, how she was barely giving me the time of day. She was just trying to protect herself from getting hurt. Who'd want to fall for something that was never meant to be real?

Why open yourself up to that kind of pain?

Oh.

A realization suddenly popped into my mind, just as I quietly rested my head against the cool surface of her bedroom door.

Maybe I wanted Simone to be falling for me...

Because I was already falling for her.

Shit. No wonder I was being so weird about her pulling away from me.

"Simone? Simone?" I knocked on her door, eager to talk to her. I needed to get to the bottom of whatever was happening between us, even if it meant hurting myself in the process.

I just needed to know how Simone felt about me–if she felt anything at all.

There was no response from the other side of the door. I tried the doorknob and was surprised when it opened with zero resistance.

The sound of running water came from the bathroom. Simone was in the shower.

Great.

I'd just have to keep waiting to have a conversation with her. I moved toward her bed and sat on the edge of it.

I had no intention of leaving her bedroom without getting her to talk to me, to at least admit that she'd been distancing herself these past few days—

Her phone vibrated near my leg on the bed, drawing my eyes. The screen was lighting up with text message after text message.

I didn't mean to snoop on her, but the messages were coming fast. When I saw Jace's name, I couldn't look away.

JACE: can't stop thinking about u

JACE: we're so perfect together baby

JACE: can't wait to have u back in my arms

The last text message contained an internet link. At first glance, it looked like it was a link to a fertility clinic.

I sprang to my feet, my heart thumping so hard I could hear it in my ears.

She's talking to Jace again?

My vision turned red as my emotions swirled around me. I felt sick to my stomach.

I'd never been more hurt. And I'd never been more pissed off. All at the same time.

"Harry?"

I looked up to see Simone standing in front of me, wrapped up in a towel. "What are you doing here?"

"Is this why you've been avoiding me?" I bit out. "Because you're going back to him?"

"Harry, what are you talking about—"

"I saw the text messages, Simone." I gestured to the phone on the bed. "Fuck! It all makes sense. No wonder you've been so different lately. It's because you're fucking cheating on me—"

"Cheating on you?" Simone narrowed her eyes. "Are you accusing me of going back on our agreement? Are you seriously accusing me of being a *cheater*?"

"I don't know." I let out a broken laugh. "I don't know who you are, Simone. I don't think I've ever known."

"You know me, Harry—"

"No, I don't." I shook my head. "Because the Simone I knew would never go back to Jace. Not after how he treated you."

"Go back to Jace?" Simone squinted in confusion. "Wait. Did you say that you saw my text messages? Harry, were you going through my phone?"

"I wasn't going through your phone. The messages just popped up on your screen—"

"And you read them? Without my permission?" She took a step closer to me. "How could you think that's okay?"

"The same way you think it's okay to go running back to that asshole—"

"Why do you care?" Simone pressed, her voice rising. "Even if I was thinking up some kind of master plan to get back with Jace, why does it matter to you? This marriage is a sham, right? This will all be over in a few weeks."

Our eyes met, and it was like a knife in my chest.

She blinked, and her next words came out softer. "None of this is real. Isn't that what you kept telling me?"

All of my anger melted away as sadness flowed through my veins instead.

None of this is real.

Fuck.

Simone didn't want me. She never wanted me. Not really.

If I was falling in love, I was falling completely alone.

"Good night, Simone." I ended the conversation as I turned away from her. "I'll see you in the morning."

24

SIMONE

Why the hell was Harry in my room last night?

I hadn't followed him out or asked any questions. I'd been too pissed off.

It was bad enough that he'd been snooping while I was in the shower. It was even worse to deal with him accusing me of cheating on him.

That was the part that hurt the most.

How could Harry believe something like that?

He knew that Jace had broken my heart. And if he'd bothered to read the text message history, he would've noticed that I literally never responded whenever Jace had occasionally texted me. The man had been in a one-person conversation with himself for months, messaging me every so often when he was lonely and bored. He never meant a word he said in those text messages, anyway.

I had zero interest in Jace. But Harry wouldn't listen to me. He'd just jumped to the worst possible conclusion about me.

I flopped down on my mattress, my thoughts racing so fast I could barely catch them.

Was it sex? Is that all Harry wanted last night?

I frowned at the thought. Just the idea of Harry coming to my bedroom to fool around and then accusing me of cheating on him made something in my stomach turn.

What an asshole.

I'd asked him right to his face if anything between us was real, and he'd never even bothered to answer the question. Which was fine by me, since I had no intention of ever sleeping with Harry, ever again.

I was completely done with him. Once and for all.

Because if there wasn't anything real between us, then it was time we started acting like it.

"You sure you're good here, Mom?" I asked as I helped her settle into her guesthouse for the night. "I can always call off the dinner with Ruby if you need me to stay."

"Simi." My mom playfully rolled her eyes. "I can still take care of myself, you know. I'm not completely helpless."

"I never said anything about you being helpless." I chuckled. "I really don't think that word describes you at all."

It was the weekend before my mom's surgery, and my nerves were totally shot. I was trying to put on a brave front for her sake, but I had a feeling she was able to see right through it.

It didn't help that I hadn't talked to Harry in days. We'd gone from short conversations to zero conversations, pretty much ignoring each other in the halls. The home had a certain coldness to it nowadays, something else I was hoping my mom hadn't picked up on.

The Wedding Hoax

"I'm going to be okay, sweetie. You go out. Have a nice dinner." My mom smiled. "And tell Ruby I said hello."

I bent to kiss my mom on the forehead before I replied, "I will. Get some good sleep, okay? I love you."

"I love you, too." My mom motioned for me to get out of her hair. "Now, go! You don't want to be late for dinner. It's rude."

I left the guesthouse and went straight to my bedroom closet. It didn't take me long to change into a sleek velvet jumpsuit. It was a modern, sexy look that I didn't want my mom seeing me in, especially since there was a deep slit in the front of it. I typically didn't go for super sexy looks, but with the pregnancy, I knew that my sexy jumpsuit days were numbered, and I wanted to take the outfit out for one last ride.

Plus, since I was going out with Ruby, I wanted to at least attempt to keep up with her. Sitting across from a woman who looked like a supermodel was going to be hard enough, but if I didn't bring my clothing A-game, it was going to be even worse.

Twenty minutes later, I was walking through the front door of the restaurant. It was an upscale place, with low lighting and chandeliers. When I said Ruby's name to the hostess, she walked me to a table near the back of the restaurant, separated from the rest of the crowd.

"Of course Ruby got us the VIP treatment." I laughed to myself as I took a seat. "Everything about that woman is luxury at its finest."

I reached for a menu as I got comfortable, looking over dinner options that all seemed to be various French cuisine entrees. The restaurant also had a rather extensive wine list, right alongside the French food that I could never hope to pronounce correctly.

"Simone?"

Harry's voice floated over to me. I looked up at him with shock. "Harry? What are you doing here?"

"I could ask you the same thing." He scoffed as he took his seat across from me. "What is this? I'm supposed to be meeting with Sean."

"Wrong. I'm supposed to be meeting with Ruby," I corrected him. "She said she wanted to catch up over dinner — Wait. I think she's texting me right now."

Ruby: Don't be mad! Sean and I just wanted you two to squash whatever's been going on with you.

Ruby: Your mom said you two haven't been talking? We were just concerned. That's the only reason we set this dinner up for you and Harry.

Ruby: LOVE YOU, PLEASE DON'T BE MAD

"Seriously?" Harry and I said the phrase at the same time. He'd been looking down at his phone, too.

"Did Sean just send you a text about what's going on?"

"Sure did." Harry scoffed again. "What? Do they think this is a movie or something? You can't just set people up on a dinner date and hope everything works out for the best."

"Oh. Sean called this a date?"

"Pretty romantic spot for it not to be." Harry groaned. "But it's not like we had a choice in having dinner here tonight."

"It's kind of sweet. Very annoying, definitely, but still sweet," I replied. "So, what do you think? Should we try to get through dinner?"

"If we don't, I'm pretty sure they'll just set us up again." Harry picked up the menu in front of him, but he paused to shamelessly look me up and down. "Uh, you look—is that what you were going to wear? When it was just you and Ruby?"

"Why? Do you think I brought a change of clothes just in case it was you instead?" I joked. "Sorry to burst your bubble, Harry O'Donnell, but I don't plan every minute of my life around you."

Harry grinned. "There she is."

I almost grinned right back, but I fought against the urge. It was too easy to fall back into a pattern with Harry, and if I wasn't careful, he'd be right back in my bed.

Which couldn't happen under any circumstances. Not just because I was pregnant, but because it was obvious that he wasn't looking for a real connection here.

Why would I let myself keep falling for someone if I was the only one with feelings?

"No." I shook my head. "We're not doing that anymore."

"Doing what?"

"That thing where you try to charm me out of acting like anything's wrong."

"I thought we were just trying to get through dinner?" Harry replied. "We can't even pretend to be nice to each other for one meal?"

"Fine. You're right." I faked a smile. "Let's pretend. Let's get through the meal."

I linked my hands together as I rested them against the table. "How's work been going for you lately? Are you almost done with the next issue of *LA Now*?"

"The publication deadline is fast approaching, so we'll have to be done sooner rather than later."

"Right. I'm sure you're ready to be done with those long hours in the office."

"I think everyone's ready for the long hours to be over—"

"Are you cheating on me, Harry?"

"Wait. What?" Harry seemed taken aback by the question. "Simone, where is that coming from?"

"You're working those long hours, right?" I pressed. "That's the same thing Jace would tell me, that he was working long hours at the office. It turned out, though, that he wasn't working long hours. Instead, he was spending all that time with a woman he'd met on a dating app."

"Simone—"

"Hold on. I haven't gotten to the best part," I cut him off. "The best part is that after I found out Jace was cheating on me, he told me that it was my fault. That because I couldn't have kids naturally, I'd ruined his dream of having a family. So, really, I should be grateful that he just hooked up with a random woman instead of just calling off our whole relationship."

"Simone, I'm so sorry—"

"Sorry for what, Harry? Cheating on me?"

"How could you even think I'm doing that?" Harry's tone was defensive. "You really think I'm anything like your asshole of an ex?"

"Turnabout is fair play, isn't it? You thought I was cheating on you, right? Do you like how it feels when I randomly accuse you of something horrible, Harry?"

"Because I saw your texts with Jace—"

"Because you snooped through my phone, Harry. Because you jumped to conclusions."

"What was I supposed to think, Simone?"

"You were supposed to talk to me!" My voice shook as painful memories of my last fight with Jace flooded my brain. "You were supposed to trust me. What are we even—"

I took a moment to calm down, my hands now pressed flat against the table. "Maybe it would just be better if we weren't anything to each other."

"What are you saying right now, Simone?"

"Why can't we cheat on each other?" I helplessly shrugged. "Why can't you stay late at the office with some sexy secretary? Why does it matter? It's not real. It's not anything. It's not even really cheating. If anything, it's a breach of contract—"

"Mr. and Mrs. O'Donnell." A waitress was suddenly grinning down at us. "Are you ready for me to take your order? Or did you need a little bit more time?"

"I think we're actually ready for the check," Harry replied, his eyes locked on mine the whole time he spoke.

25

HARRY

I'd lost my appetite at the dinner table.

We were sharing a cab ride back home, but there was no sign of life inside the car. Simone hadn't said a word to me since we'd gotten the check.

And I couldn't think of anything to say to her, either.

Why can't we cheat on each other?

The question was rolling around in my mind, gaining traction with each turn. There was something burning in the back of my brain, too, every time I looked over at her.

I needed to say something.

I knew that, but instead, I just pushed everything down. I didn't want to be the first one to put their cards on the table, only to have Simone tell me that she wasn't even interested in playing cards. It didn't help that she hadn't mentioned feeling anything for me, at all. Even when it looked like she was about to cry during dinner, it seemed like she was more upset about being called a cheater than the idea of actually cheating.

Shit.

I needed to apologize about that. If I didn't say anything

else tonight, the least I needed to do was tell her sorry for jumping to conclusions. I mentally rehearsed my apology, playing it on repeat in my head as we pulled up to the house. Once we were inside, I followed behind her, intent on walking her all the way to her bedroom.

As soon as we reached it, she quickly tried to open her door.

But I pulled it shut, keeping us both in the hall. "Simone. I'm sorry—"

"What if I was?"

"What?"

"What if I was cheating on you?" Simone stared at me. "How would that make you feel?"

"Simone, we have a contract. If anyone found out that you were sleeping with someone else while we're married, it would be in violation of—"

"What if I invited him over and slept with him in my bed?"

"Simone, what are you—"

"How would that make you feel, Harry?" Simone moved closer. "If I was with somebody else in the same bed that I've been with you in?"

I felt something in my blood start to boil. "Don't."

"Don't what?"

"Don't say things you don't mean just to piss me off."

"So, that's how you'd feel, then? Pissed off?"

"One hundred percent," I said.

"Why?"

"Because you're *mine*, Simone. That's why. And as long as you're married to me, no one else gets to touch you the way that I touch you."

"Not even Jace?"

"You're playing a dangerous game right now, Simone." I

pressed my body against hers, until her back was to the door.

"I never said I was playing a game." Her words were low as she gently brushed her fingers along the underside of my jaw. She was quiet for a moment before she whispered again, "Show me."

"Show you what?"

"Show me how no one else is supposed to touch me." Simone's hand trailed down my chest.

But I moved her hand away from me, right before I reached for her hips. A few seconds later and I'd lifted Simone high enough for her to wrap her legs around my waist in return.

I wildly kissed down her chest as I pressed her against her bedroom door. She groaned underneath me, and I brought a hand up toward the front of her jumpsuit, exploring her skin. It didn't take long for my fingertips to find her sensitive nipples, soon circling them one after the other.

"Fuck. Harry." Simone groaned again, just as I took one of her nipples between my lips.

I ran my tongue across it rhythmically, keeping in time with the moans coming from her throat. She wrapped her arms behind my head, like she wanted to make sure I stayed right there. As I continued moving my mouth against her chest, I felt my cock straining against the fabric of my pants.

Fuck.

I wanted her. And I wanted her *now*.

I reached for the doorknob to her bedroom, casually opening it with Simone still wrapped around me. A few seconds later, I placed her down on the bed. Just as eager as I was, Simone started to quickly undress, letting her jumpsuit slip down to the bed. Her hands moved toward her panties next, but I was faster.

I pulled them down to the bedroom floor, right before I settled between her thighs.

And then I brought my mouth up to her pussy.

"Harry... Harry..." Simone writhed underneath me, her hands gripping the bedsheets. "Oh my God..."

I licked her clit in small, fast circles, with one of my fingers playing with her entrance. When I could tell she was wet enough, I slipped that same finger inside of her, my tongue still working her at the same time. I groaned when I felt her pussy tightening around my finger, letting me know she was about to go over the edge.

"Not yet, baby. Not yet," I said as I moved away from her, my hands pulling off the rest of my clothes. I moved back toward her, grabbing her thighs before I lined my cock up with her pussy. It didn't take me long to sink myself inside of her, my hands reaching for her own as I hovered over her.

"You're mine," I reminded her as I thrust my cock even deeper. "You're all mine, Simone."

"Yours..." She wrapped her legs around me, keeping me in place inside of her. "I'm all yours, Harry."

After she spoke, it felt like something broke loose inside of me. I couldn't contain myself anymore and increased my pace, moving against her even faster and even harder than before. She whimpered underneath me, her pussy already tightening around my cock.

And then she was coming, hard and fast.

"That's right, baby. Come for me," I groaned, feeling my cock starting to spill into her pussy, too. "Fuck. That feels so fucking good, Simone."

I groaned again as I finished inside of her, soon collapsing beside her body. Our fingers were still intertwined as we caught our breath, our chests heaving in time with each other's. Somewhere in the quiet, a thought slid into my head, one that I wasn't able to shake no matter how much I tried.

Was Simone actually mine?

The thought haunted the back of my mind as I looked over at her. Her eyes were closed, with a small smile playing at her lips.

Sure, our sex had been great. It was always great between us.

But had tonight just been about sex? It was almost like she wanted me to claim her, like she wanted to make me jealous just by mentioning her ex asshole's name.

But was this just a game to her?

Fuck.

Maybe having sex now was going to make everything else so much worse.

It certainly wasn't going to help when it came to letting her go, which was supposed to happen in a few weeks' time. How the hell was I supposed to let Simone go?

I wanted her more than I'd ever wanted anything.

All I wanted was for her to stay.

"Simone?" My voice was low. "You still awake?"

"Mm-hmm." She nodded, even though her eyes were still closed. "Barely. Why? You weren't trying to go for another round, were you?"

My heart sank inside my chest. "No. This wasn't about that."

"Oh. There was something else you wanted to talk to me about?"

I want you to be with me. I want you to stay.

I want this to be real.

"Nope. I was just checking in," I lied. "You know how it is

sometimes when things get intense. I wanted to make sure you were okay with everything."

"More than okay." She lightly chuckled. "Some might say I even prefer it that way."

I pressed a gentle kiss against her shoulder. "Good. Glad to hear I delivered, then."

"You always do." Simone tightly squeezed my hand. "Okay. I think I'm going to pass out. Good night, Harry."

"Good night, Simone." I squeezed her hand back, not wanting to let go of any part of her.

Not wanting this night to end. Especially if it was going to be one of our last.

26

SIMONE

*L*ast night was *weird*.

Being with Harry again felt just like old times, when we'd fall into each other's beds like it was nothing. But it'd also felt different, like there was something unspoken between us, something we were trying to express without saying a word.

There was a heaviness to everything that I hadn't been expecting.

It didn't help that we were technically still in a fight. He'd never fully apologized for accusing me of cheating with Jace. Which meant that despite our night together, I still needed to hold my ground.

I couldn't let Harry just fuck me and assume I'd forgive him for anything.

Nope. No way.

I took a deep breath as I finished getting dressed for the day. I was wearing a jean dress I'd pulled out the back of my closet, its fabric ending at my knees. I wasn't sure if jean dresses were back in fashion or still considered a no-no, but I wasn't really in the mood to care.

The Wedding Hoax

With my mom's surgery coming up soon, my nerves were way too shot to care about being fashionable.

"Harry?" I said his name like a question as I walked into the living room. I was confused since I spotted a large picnic basket and blanket laid out on a nearby table.

And then, something burned inside of me.

What the hell? Is Harry going out on a date?

After all the crap he gave me about cheating with Jace? After the night we'd just had?

"Harry?" I called his name again, now wanting answers. He needed to explain himself or else I was going to—

"Hey." Harry suddenly greeted me with a warm smile. He was dressed down, just wearing a T-shirt and dark jeans. "There you are. I was just about to come find you."

"Why? To let me know about your plans?" I scoffed. "I can't believe you. Seriously. Have fun on your date—"

"Date?" Harry looked confused for a moment.

Then his face lit up with laughter. "Sorry. I just—yeah, I can see how you might think I'm going on a date. But no. I'm actually going on a picnic."

"By yourself?"

"With you and Eileen," he replied. "I thought it'd be something nice to do. Maybe help take your minds off her big surgery coming up."

Oh.

The anger inside of me quickly melted as I smiled back at him. "That's really nice of you, Harry. Thanks."

"Yeah, I figured it's the least I could do." He nodded with a small smile. "I'm also kind of hoping it counts as an apology?"

He took a step closer to me before he went on. "I'm really sorry about everything I said about you and Jace. I'm sorry for looking at your phone. I'm sorry for just generally being an asshole recently. I wish I could blame work but..." He shrugged. "I don't think it had anything to do with work. I think it was just about me feeling insecure."

"Insecure?"

"It's just a stupid guy thing. I know we're not really married, but we still are, you know? We are to everybody else. And I think it was just driving me crazy, the idea of you being with someone else."

"Because you didn't want other people to think I'd cheat on you?"

"Because I didn't want other people to think you'd ever be with him," he corrected. "That you'd ever choose someone like him over me. Especially since he already hurt you. Imagine what kind of guy I must be, right? If you were willing to go back to Jace."

"Yeah. Imagine." I playfully rolled my eyes. "Because it's never going to happen. Ever. I'm done with Jace, Harry. I mean it."

"I know." Harry bent to gently press a kiss against my lips. "I'm sorry for making such a huge deal out of nothing."

"Apology accepted." I smiled against the kiss as warmth bloomed inside my chest.

"You're dressed perfectly, by the way." He looked at my outfit, scanning it up and down. "Almost like you already knew about the picnic somehow."

"Nope. Not a mind reader. Just a girl who wanted to be comfortable." I beamed. "All right. Let me go get my mom before we head out—"

"I can get her." Harry held up a hand. "Why don't you just wait right here?"

"Uh, all right?" I was so shocked all I could do was stand still.

Harry was going to help my mom get over here from the guesthouse?

Huh.

I suddenly had a feeling that today was going to be filled with surprises.

~

"It's such a nice day for a picnic," my mom said as we headed toward the middle of the park.

She was right. It was a bright, sunny day in LA, and it seemed like everyone got the memo. The park was full of kids skateboarding on the sidewalk, couples sharing ice cream cones as they walked their dogs, and older people out for a leisurely stroll. It was nice seeing everyone out like this, though, almost like getting a snapshot of the perfect day in LA.

Harry was busy setting up a spot for us to sit. He'd also brought an oversized umbrella, which I watched him set up to give my mom some cover from the sun. It was so thoughtful and so sweet that I barely knew how to respond to it.

He was acting like he was actually my husband.

Like we were actually part of a family. I mean, in a way, I guess we would be family soon enough. I was carrying his baby, after all, even though I still hadn't broken the news to him about it.

Crap.

I really needed to find the right time to tell him.

"Is that good, Eileen? Do you have enough cover?" Harry asked. "I can always move the umbrella over if you think—"

"No, no. It's good, Harry. Thank you." My mom smiled at him. "For everything."

"How about you, Simone?" He turned toward me after we'd both settled down on the blanket. "You good?"

"I'm great." I offered him a quick wink. "Thanks for putting this together, Harry—"

My words were cut off by a frisbee zipping right between us.

"Hey! My frisbee!" a young kid called out.

"My dog! Oh my God! He just got away from me!" an older woman called out, too.

"Dog?" It was the last thing I said before a golden retriever bounded right past us, too. Quickly putting two and two together, I realized that the dog and the frisbee were unrelated. The owner of the dog hadn't thrown the frisbee but the dog had chased after it, anyway.

And now, the dog was almost halfway across the park.

"Be right back!" I jumped into action, chasing after the stranger's dog. I'd noticed it had a leash still attached to it, so it shouldn't have been too hard to grab on to him.

As I ran across the park, I noticed that someone was running right next to me, keeping up with my every step.

Harry.

"Are we seriously chasing after a dog right now?" he asked, his legs still pumping. "I feel like we're in some kind of movie."

"Someone's gotta do it!" I let out a breezy laugh as we continued to run. "Come on! We almost got him!"

A few moments later, the dog's leash was within my grasp. My fingers wrapped around the blue fabric just as the dog pulled the frisbee into his mouth. Before I knew it, the dog was headed back in the opposite direction, moving so fast that I could barely keep up with him.

"Harry!" I yelled out for help, my feet struggling to stay on the ground. "Help!"

"I've got it! I've got you!" Harry said as he tried to take the leash out of my hand. Unfortunately, his attempt to free me only made things worse as the fabric soon wrapped his wrist. We were both trapped now, helplessly chasing behind a dog who was taking us wherever he wanted to go.

"Stay, boy! Stay!" I tried and failed to instruct the golden retriever. "Uh, heel? Heel!"

The dog ignored me as it took a sharp turn. Its movements freed us from its leash, and I watched as it ran back up to its owner with the frisbee still in its mouth. Although, in that same moment, it felt like I was falling—

Probably because I *was* falling—

And a second or two later, I was lying on top of Harry, who'd also fallen to the ground after the dog had unintentionally set us free. We locked eyes for a moment before bursting into a shared laugh as we rested on the grass.

"I cannot believe that just happened," I said, still laughing.

"No good deed goes unpunished." Harry was still laughing, too. He smiled up at me as he brought a hand up to the side of my face. "You look beautiful, you know. Even when you're being dragged to within an inch of your life by a dog."

"I think that's the most bizarre compliment I've ever gotten in my life." I smirked. "But thank you. You didn't look too bad yourself."

Harry chuckled before he brought my head down toward his own, gently kissing me for the second time today. And just like the first time, my heart warmed at the feeling of his lips against mine.

∼

"Did you actually make these sandwiches?" I said as I finished up my lunch. We were still sitting in the park as a calm breeze washed over our skin. "Not that I'm questioning your abilities in the kitchen—"

"You just didn't think I had any abilities in the kitchen?" Harry grinned. "You wouldn't be wrong. For the most part. I tend to order out or have food catered because it's more convenient. But I know my way around a slice of bread and some choice condiments."

"I believe you." I looked up at my mom, eyeing the rest of her meal. She only had a few bites left to go. "Mom? Do you like your lunch?"

"Yes. It's delicious. Thank you, Harry." My mom wistfully sighed. "I haven't had a picnic in such a long time. Not since Simi's dad was still with us."

"Is anyone feeling ice cream?" Harry looked between my mom and me. "I think they also have churros, if that's more your speed."

"Ice cream!" Mom and I answered in unison.

"Chocolate? Vanilla? Strawberry?"

"Surprise us," Mom said, and I nodded.

"Will do." Harry stood up from the blanket. I watched him walk to the parking lot, where food trucks were parked along the street.

My mom looked over at me with an expression I couldn't read on her face.

"What?" I pressed. "What is it?"

"I think I was wrong, Simi."

"Wrong?"

"I was wrong to have ever been worried about you and Harry." She grinned. "I knew there was a romance brewing between you but after what I've seen today? I never should've doubted your relationship. Ever."

"Mom—"

"And look at what he did for us with the picnic," she went on. "I think you're bringing out another side of him, Simi. When we first met, he seemed so different. More closed off. But this? This is absolutely wonderful."

"Mom, I just—" I took a deep breath as I tried to find my words. "Can we not talk about this right now?"

"Why not?"

"Because it's not important." I shook my head. "Because making sure you're feeling okay before your surgery is what really matters. It's the only reason Harry did all this, anyway."

"Another reason he'd be a good pick—"

"Mom," I playfully scoffed. "It's like you're not listening to a word I'm saying!"

"I'm hearing every word you're saying, Simi." She beamed. "But that doesn't mean I don't have the right to speak my mind."

"What are you two talking about?" Harry asked as he returned to the picnic blanket. He handed me a strawberry ice cream cone before he handed my mom a chocolate one. "I hope it wasn't about how neither one of you is really in the mood for ice cream, because I don't think that place does refunds."

"Nothing," I said as I took the cone into my hand. "We weren't talking about anything."

"Really?"

"Really." I shared a quick look with my mom who nodded in agreement.

Phew.

Awkward bullet successfully dodged.

27

SIMONE

Monday morning.

I was slow to get out of bed, terrified to get the day started. It was the day of my mom's surgery, and I didn't know how I was going to handle it if things somehow went wrong.

If the surgery failed and she didn't gain back any of her mobility? Fine.

But if the surgery failed and my mom didn't make it home?

I could barely process the thought, my body on the verge of trembling with fear.

My mom was all I had left.

I somehow managed to drag myself out of bed, even though with every step, I felt something turning over in my stomach. I tried to eat breakfast, but everything tasted wrong, like it needed more sugar or more salt or more *something*.

My mom seemed fine, though. She was sipping on a glass of water since she had to fast before her surgery.

"Are you feeling okay?" I asked as I looked over at her.

The Wedding Hoax

"Did you need me to get you anything?"

"I'm fine." She smiled. "Are you feeling okay? You look like you barely got any sleep."

"That's because I barely did."

"Simi."

"Mom." I faked a smile. "I think it's okay if I'm worried about you."

"You don't need to be worried about me. I'll be okay."

"But you don't know that for sure."

"Just like you don't know for sure that I won't be okay." She lightly chuckled as she spoke. "And yet, you're so convinced that the worst thing is always going to happen."

"I just want you to be okay," I murmured. "I *need* you to be okay, Mom."

"Is everyone ready to go?" Harry asked as he stepped into the room. "Eileen? Are you ready? Simone?"

I tilted my head to the side in confusion. "You're talking like you're coming with us."

"That's because I *am*."

"You're not going to work?" I shook my head. "I thought you had to stay on top of the next release of *LA Now*."

"I do. And I am. But I can still make time for what's important."

"Okay. As long as you're sure..." My words trailed off. "Well, in that case, yeah. I think we're all ready to go."

"Great. I'll call the car."

~

"Mom? Wait," I pleaded with her right before she finished checking into the hospital for her surgery. "Just—hold on."

We'd arrived at the hospital a few minutes early, with

Harry standing behind my mom's wheelchair as I trailed behind them both. I was too anxious to pretend like I wasn't, but I also didn't want my energy rubbing off on my mom.

Except right now, I didn't care about any bad energy. As I watched a nurse come to bring my mom back into the surgery room, something snapped inside of me.

"I love you, Mom," I said as I reached down toward her and pulled her in for a tight hug. "I love you so much."

"I love you, too, Simi." She returned my hug, her arms comforting and warm. "And I'll see you in a little bit."

I nodded before I let her go. The nurse offered me a small smile before she ushered her into the back of the hospital, their frames soon disappearing down the hallway.

I felt Harry's hand reaching for my own, and he folded his palm into mine.

"She's going to be okay." His voice was low. "This is the best hospital in the state. Hell, I think it's one of the best hospitals in the world."

"That doesn't matter." My words shook as I spoke. "Sometimes things go wrong and there's nothing anyone can do for you. I was up all last night reading about how easy it is for spinal surgery to go wrong, how easy it is to mess it all up—"

"Walk with me."

"What?"

"Walk with me," he repeated. "I'm a little hungry, and I'm pretty sure I saw a few vending machines down this way."

"Okay." I was thrown off by the sudden change in conversation, but I still walked with him. We didn't stop until we reached a row of vending machines, the hospital's lights reflecting off their glass.

"What was your favorite snack? When you were a kid?" Harry asked as he stared at one of the machines.

I thought about the question for a moment before I responded, "Sour cream and onion pretzels."

"What?" Harry's eyes went wide. "Your favorite snack as a kid was pretzels?"

"What's so wrong with that?"

"Everything!" Harry laughed as he shook his head. "That's like saying your favorite snack as a kid was popcorn."

"I mean, popcorn is pretty good."

"Whatever." Harry chuckled again. "My favorite snack when I was a kid, just for the record, was dipping barbecue chips in queso. Because if you're going to eat an unhealthy snack, you might as well commit."

"Gross." I frowned. "That sounds like it'd be a salt bomb in your mouth."

"Uh, you're the one eating sour cream and onion pretzels. I don't think you get to judge anyone when it comes to salt bombs in their mouths."

"Yeah, but my salt bomb was delicious." I smirked. "And that makes all the difference."

Harry smirked back before he pulled out his wallet. He then swiped a card against the vending machine's reader and punched his selections in the keypad.

I watched as a few items fell inside the window—a bag of pretzels, followed by a bag of barbecue chips, followed by two bottled waters. When everything was said and done, Harry grabbed for the treasure trove of snacks, then motioned toward me.

"Let's head back to the lobby."

∿

*H*arry and I sat side by side as we waited for any updates on my mom's surgery.

I'd practically inhaled my pretzels in the meantime, downing the bottle of water soon after.

It was hard to concentrate on anything, my brain foggy with worry. The only thing I could think about was my mom on the operating table and whether or not the surgeon knew what they were doing in there—

"Hey." Harry's voice cut through the noise in my brain.

"Hey." I offered him a small wave. "How's it going?"

"Pretty good, considering you never offered me a single pretzel." He smirked. "I was just about to offer you a few chips but by the time I looked back over, all the pretzels were gone."

"Sorry."

"No need to apologize." He waved a hand between us. "I'm just happy that you were able to actually eat something. I was worried about you."

"You were worried about me?"

"Yeah. I had a feeling you didn't eat anything for breakfast. And with how you've been so laser-focused on your mom this morning... I just wanted to make sure you had everything you needed."

"Thanks." I let out a tired sigh. "You're right. I have been kind of all over the place. Or I guess, stuck in one place."

"It's hard. Caring about people. You always run the risk of getting hurt."

"That's why you mostly avoid it, right?" I joked. "Except for Paul. And maybe your family, but only on a really good day."

"And you," Harry added, his eyes locked on mine. "I care about you, Simone. And I think I always will."

And I think I always will.

I wanted to say something, but I struggled to find the right words. Was Harry really saying that he was going to care about me, even when this was all over?

Even when the jig was finally up?

"Excuse me? Mrs. O'Donnell?" A nurse was now standing in front of me with a clipboard in her hand. "I just wanted to give you an update on your mom."

"Is everything okay?" My heart was racing fast, like it was going to leap out of my chest at any moment.

"Yes, everything's fine." The nurse smiled down at me. "Your mother was just put to sleep and she's reacting normally to the procedure so far. Typically, the surgery takes a few hours. We just like to let the family know in case you need to leave and come back later—"

"I'm not going anywhere," I cut her off. "I'm going to wait right here."

"Do you have a lobby where I'd be able to plug in my laptop?" Harry asked. "Just in case I needed to catch up on some work?"

"Yes. We have a visitors' area right down the hall." The nurse nodded. "And please, let us know if you need anything else, okay?"

As she walked away, I watched Harry shuffle out of his seat next to me.

"I'm going to head to the visitors' area, if you want to come with me?" He started. "I need to catch up on what's going on with the magazine's release."

"I think I'd rather stay here."

"Are you sure?" Harry frowned. "Because I don't know if you should be alone right now—"

"I'm not alone. You're going to be right down the hall, right?"

"Right." Harry was still staring at me, his face filled with concern. "All right, then. Just let me know if you need me and I'll come running right back—"

"I'll let you know. I promise."

28

SIMONE

"How's our girl doing?" Harry asked as he knelt down in front of me. He rested one of his arms against my thighs as he crouched close to me. "Is she out of surgery yet?"

It'd been a few hours since I'd seen Harry, even though the time had flown by. I was so anxious and numb that time didn't have much of a meaning to me anymore.

"She just got out," I said with my hands folded in my lap. "They said she's in recovery mode now."

"Is she awake?"

"Not yet."

"Do they know when she'll wake up?"

"Maybe in another hour or so? But she might not be in the mood to talk." I shrugged. "Either way, I'll probably be sleeping at the hospital tonight."

"Got it. In that case, we'll need to start thinking about dinner plans. I don't think we can have anything delivered, but I can pick us up something to eat when I'm done working and bring it back here."

"Ha." There was a shadow of a smile on my lips. "You make it sound like we're having a sleepover."

"Aren't we?" Harry quirked an eyebrow. "Or is there somewhere else you wanted me to sleep tonight?"

"You don't have to do that, Harry."

"I know I don't have to, Simone. I want to." He gently tapped the side of my thigh. "I want to be here for you while you're going through this. And I want to be there for your mom, too."

"Stop," I whispered.

"What?"

"I mean, you should get back to work. Until it's time for dinner, and then we can figure out the rest."

"Yeah, you're right. I do need to get back to it. Some of the advertisers have been trying to schedule a call with me all morning. I'll probably go take it out in the car." Harry stood up, then leaned down to softly kiss my forehead. "Call me if you need anything?"

"Will do."

Stop. Stop. Stop.

The word repeated in my head as Harry walked out of the room.

All I wanted was for him to *stop*. To stop pretending like he was actually my husband. To stop pretending like he was always going to be there for my mom, like he was always going to be there for me.

Because if he kept going on like this, I was going to start believing him.

And as soon as I let myself completely fall for Harry, I knew that was when he'd take it all away.

∽

"Mom?" I was sitting next to my mom, my hand resting on her pillow. "Mom? Are you awake? Can you hear me?"

"I can hear you, Simi." My mom turned to look at me, her eyes still closed. "Everything feels a little heavy right now, but I can still hear you."

"How are you feeling?"

"Sore." She groaned. "But good. Mostly good."

"Great." I looked her up and down. "It doesn't look like anything's out of place."

"Oh? You mean they didn't reattach my elbow to my shoulder like I asked them to?"

"Mom."

"I'm only joking." She tried to chuckle, but it came out too low. "Where's Harry? Did he leave to go to work?"

"Actually, he's been working from the hospital all day. He even took a work call out in the parking lot."

"He's been at the hospital this whole time?"

"He said he wanted to be here for us." I nodded. "And the only reason he's not here right now is because he's out picking up dinner."

"Such a good husband." My mom let out a heavy breath. "Your dad would've done the same thing for me."

"Did the surgeon mention anything? About your mobility?" I changed the subject, not wanting to think about Harry in that way right now. I wanted to focus on one crisis at a time, and right now my mom's health felt like the most pressing issue.

"Yes. He mentioned that I'm going to need physical rehab for a while," she started. "But he thinks my chance to regain my mobility is really high. He said I should be able to go from using my wheelchair to using crutches, maybe even a walker someday."

"Mom! That's amazing!"

"Isn't it?" She shifted in her hospital bed. "It's such amazing news that I can hardly believe it."

"I'm so happy for you." I felt tears welling behind my eyes as I spoke.

"Don't cry, Simi. There's no reason for tears."

"How can you tell I'm crying? Your eyes aren't even open!"

"A mother always knows." She tried to chuckle again. "I can hear it in your voice. I always know exactly how you're feeling."

She paused for a moment before she continued. "It's why I can tell how conflicted you are about Harry, too."

"Can we talk about something else? Please? Literally, anything else."

"It's okay to be conflicted," Mom reassured me. "Life is full of difficult choices. It's hard to know who you can trust. It's even harder to trust someone with your heart. You should take your time."

"Thanks, Mom." I smiled over at her, even though she couldn't see me. "I'll keep thinking about it, okay?"

"Dinner is served!" Harry announced as he stepped into the hospital room. "I had to go to three different places just to find those sushi rolls you wanted. Seems like cooked salmon is in high demand for a dinner option."

Harry looked over at my mom, a huge grin forming on his face. "Eileen! How are you feeling?"

"She's good," I answered on her behalf, wanting to save her the effort. "Recovering. And her mobility prospects after physical therapy look really good, too."

"That's great to hear," Harry said while placing a takeout

bag on the table in the room. He then held up two bottles of sparkling apple cider. "I got these as sort of a surprise. I was thinking we could toast? If all went well?"

"You want to toast with apple cider?" I tried to keep my expression blank, even as my anxiety spiked through the roof.

Oh my God.

Is that why Harry was being so nice to me lately?

Did he already know about the baby?

"I figured your mom couldn't drink anything with alcohol in it, because of the pain meds." He moved closer to the bed. "But I didn't want that to stop the celebration."

"Always thinking about other people." My mom sighed. "Such a good husband."

"Well, not that great of a husband since it looks like I completely forgot the glasses." Harry grimaced.

"We can just drink from the bottles." I pulled one out of his grip. "I don't think my mom is in the right headspace for a toast, anyway."

"Yeah, I think she just fell asleep." Harry laughed. "God. Those pain meds are going to have her knocked out all the time."

Harry clinked his bottle against mine. "Cheers to your mom's surgery going off without a hitch."

"Cheers." I clinked my bottle against his, too. "And thanks for everything. Being here. Getting dinner. All of it."

"You're very welcome." Harry opened his bottle of cider before he took a long swig. "Hmm. Apple cider might not be as delicious as champagne, but it's still pretty good in a pinch."

"Are you still going to stay the night?" I tried to be casual about it as I opened my bottle. "Because it looks like there's only one couch."

"Yeah, but I think we can make enough space for both of us."

I nodded and took a drink from the bottle, trying not to get lost in his eyes.

We ate our dinner as my mom slept on her bed. I was ravenous, and I finished quickly.

Soon, we were both snuggled up on the couch for the evening.

"Are you comfortable?" I asked as I practically lay on top of him.

"Pretty comfortable, yeah." Harry pulled me even closer. "I'm surprised you haven't passed out yet."

"Why? Because I ordered like four rolls of sushi?"

"No, because today's been so stressful for you. I just assumed it would've gotten to you by now."

"I think I'm too freaked out to sleep," I admitted. "Hospitals remind me too much of what happened to my dad. It's like I'm stuck inside of the worst night of my life all over again."

"I'm sorry you're having to relive that." Harry ran a hand through my hair, his voice soft.

"I mean, it's a little different this time." I looked up at him.

"How so?"

"You're here." I smiled. "I don't feel so alone this time around."

My face fell, just then, as a realization hit me. "Or is that completely pathetic? That I'm leaning on you so hard during something like this? Especially with how busy you are? And the fact that we're not even—"

"I'm happy that you're leaning on me," Harry interrupted. "And I'm happy to be here, Simone. I like that you feel less alone with me."

"I'm happy that you're here, too." It was the last thing I said before I closed my eyes, surrendering to the warm feeling of being pressed against him, losing myself in the moment. I rested my head against his shoulder, and sleep soon took me over.

When I woke up the next day, Harry was gone.

29

HARRY

I hadn't been to the hospital in a few days.

I'd still been in contact with Simone but after hearing her say that Eileen needed physical therapy, I knew that there was something I needed to do at home. Thankfully, the same crew who had just finished the greenhouse were willing to do some extra work around my home, too.

For a lot of extra cash, of course.

"Simone? Is that you?" I heard something at the front door and quickly went to answer it. When I pulled open the door, Simone was smiling on the other side. Eileen was right in front of her, seated in her wheelchair and still in her hospital gown.

"Sorry. I should've told you that we were coming home," Simone started. "I was going to text you, but I got so caught up in making sure everything was good before leaving the hospital."

"You don't need to give me a heads-up about you coming home." I smiled back at her. "Come on. I have a surprise for both of you."

I motioned for them to walk further into the house

before I turned down the hall. "When you told me that Eileen would need rehab, I realized that the guesthouse wouldn't be enough space for her."

"That's okay. We could always do her rehab at the hospital. Right, Mom?"

"Right. It might be a little bit of hassle, but Simi and I could make it work."

"I don't think that's fair." I shook my head as I continued to walk down the hall. "I don't think you should have to go back and forth like that, not after the kind of surgery you had."

I stopped when I reached a room with a closed door. "I think it'd be a lot easier if you could do your therapy here."

I opened the door, revealing what used to be the first-floor library. Gone were the office supplies and moving boxes I'd never bothered to open when I bought the house. Everything had been replaced by useful things, things that Eileen was going to need for her rehab. There were parallel bars to help Eileen learn how to walk again, even a small set of steps for when she was ready to try tackling those.

There was also a resting space, complete with potted plants and calming artwork on the walls. I didn't want the room to become symbolic of something painful and hard, so I'd instructed the guys who'd fixed it up and cleaned it out to make sure there was something calming in it, too.

"Harry, this is..." Simone's eyes were wide as she took in the room.

"Wonderful," Eileen said, her voice lined with awe. "Oh, Harry. It's perfect."

"You really like it?" I nervously asked. "Because if you don't like it, Eileen, we can take out or put in whatever you want."

"I love it, Harry." Eileen turned to look up at me. "You have no idea how grateful I am for this."

"I love it, too." Simone walked further into the room. "But seriously, though, how big is your house? I didn't even know this room was back here!"

"Maybe I just didn't want you roaming around my home unsupervised."

"Maybe you just didn't want me to know how much I'd be able to claim in the divorce," she joked, as she continued to look around the room. "Is this the only secret room? Or is this the part where you tell us there's like, a whole other house behind that wall?"

"Actually, I do have one more surprise for you."

Simone's mouth fell open. "Harry! I was just joking about the second house! Are you serious?"

"I mean, it's not a second house. Well, not exactly." I grinned before I turned to leave the room. "Come on! It should be waiting for us in the yard."

~

"Oh my God." It was all Simone said as we arrived in front of the greenhouse. It was bigger than the average greenhouse to accommodate Eileen's wheelchair, and hopefully in the near future, her walker. The door to the greenhouse was open, and we could already see that it was lined wall-to-wall with colorful flowers and hanging vines, every plant accessible at wheelchair height.

"Is this what they've been working on back here this whole time?" Simone gasped. "I knew it had to be something when you made us use the side entrance to the house that one time. But I just figured it was some rich guy thing."

"Some rich guy thing?" I laughed. "What rich guy thing did you think they were building in my backyard, Simone?"

"I don't know! They always kept it covered with tarps." Simone seemed to think over the question. "Maybe new parking for some fancy sports car?"

"Do I really seem like the fancy sports car type?"

"You don't *not* seem like the fancy sports car type."

Simone's mom wheeled past us as she made her way into the greenhouse. We both quietly watched as she seemed to gravitate toward a certain section, her focus sharp and intense. She picked up a potted pink rose, and she brought it up to her face.

And tears began to stream down her cheeks.

"Eileen?" I hastily walked up to her. "What's wrong? Are you in pain?"

"No. I'm not in pain." Eileen was all choked up. "It's just—Simi's dad—my husband—he would always bring me pink roses just like this. I would always plant them, too. But roses can be so fickle, and ever since I've been in a wheelchair, I haven't been able to grow them. But now..."

Eileen motioned toward both of us. "Would it be okay if you left me with these flowers? Just for a moment."

"Of course, Eileen." I grabbed Simone's hand and led us out of the greenhouse. Wanting to give Eileen as much space as she needed, we didn't stop walking until we were standing back near the main house.

"You've really outdone yourself today, Harry," Simone said as she leaned against the wall. "My mom rarely gets emotional like that. It's like you brought Dad back to her, if only for a little while."

I smiled.

Simone suddenly looked up. "Hey, why'd you build a greenhouse, anyway? I get why you built the rehab room, but you can always put that back the way it was, after my mom and I leave. But the greenhouse? Isn't that more permanent?"

"I built the greenhouse because you were mad at me."

"What?"

"I don't know. After that night in your room, when I came in but didn't really do anything? It sort of felt like you were pulling away from me. Honestly, it's felt like that off and on for the last few weeks. Like you don't want to be as close to me."

"I'm sorry I made you feel that way." She looked down at the ground. "I've just been going through a lot lately."

"I understand." I put a finger underneath her chin, forcing her to look back up at me. "There's another reason I built the greenhouse, though."

"Which was?"

"Because I want you to feel comfortable to stay as long as you want. Or as long as you need."

"Harry, you don't have to—"

"I know sometimes recovery takes longer than anyone wants it to. But I don't want you or Eileen to have to worry about that. Eileen doesn't deserve that kind of stress and neither do you."

Simone looked at me without saying a word.

Before I knew it, her lips were pressed against mine. Her body was close to my chest as she kissed me, and instinctively, I wrapped my arms around her waist. We were like that for more moments than I could count, completely lost in each other, holding each other tight.

Stay, Simone.

Stay. Stay. Stay.

I almost let the words slip out of me, but I knew better.

Even if I wanted Simone to move in with me tomorrow, there was still so much we needed to discuss.

Hell, I still didn't know if she felt the same way about me as I did about her.

I had no idea how she felt at all.

30

HARRY

"Hey." Simone was standing in the doorway of my bedroom, wearing an oversized T-shirt so long that it reached her knees.

It was nighttime now, and Simone and I hadn't spoken much since the big kiss. She'd been helping her mom get reacquainted with her guesthouse and walking her through her new medication regimen, too.

"Hey, yourself." I walked up to her and gently pulled her into the room by her waist. "I don't think I've seen you in this look before."

"That's because this is the sort of clothing I only wear when I'm alone." She laughed. "Or when I feel comfortable enough to show someone the super unpolished side of me."

"I don't know if I'd call this super unpolished." I laughed now, too. "You still look absolutely gorgeous."

Simone playfully rolled her eyes. "Anyway, I just wanted to come and thank you again for everything."

"You don't have to thank me. I did it *for* you. Not because I wanted anything from you."

"Okay, but what if I wanted to give you something,

anyway?" Simone nudged against me, pushing me back toward the mattress. "Is that allowed? Am I allowed to give you a gift, too?"

"What did you have in mind, baby?" I said just as I fell back against the bed.

"You'll see." Simone smirked, her hands going down toward the belt on my jeans. A few seconds later, she'd pulled them down to the bedroom floor, along with my boxers, too.

After that, her mouth was on my cock. She bobbed her head up and down, her mouth sliding up and down my shaft in a steady rhythm. I groaned underneath her as I felt my cock straining against her lips.

"Fuck, baby." I groaned again, just as she took even more of me down her throat. I gently placed a hand on the back of Simone's head, keeping her in place, my tip already beginning to leak with precum. "That feels so fucking good."

She began to move her mouth against me even faster, her tongue swirling all along my leaking tip. I shuddered as I felt myself about to go right over the edge, my cock as hard as a rock between her lips.

"Baby, if you keep going like that I'm going to—fuck!" I moaned as I came against her tongue, strings of my cum landing inside of her mouth. My hips moved up to meet her as she continued moving up and down my shaft, not stopping until the last drop of my cum had leaked out of my tip.

∼

"Harry! Harry!" Simone was on top of me, riding my cock to her heart's content. "Oh my God! I'm coming!"

After Simone had gone down on me, everything had

turned into a perfect sort of chaotic blur. We were all over each other and under each other. I didn't even know how long we'd been at it, just that I'd loved every single minute of it.

A few moments later, she fell beside me on the bed, her chest heaving.

"Good?" I asked just as she moved closer to me, not stopping until her head was resting on my chest.

"Amazing." She smiled before planting a small kiss against my skin. "As always."

"I think that might be a record breaker for us."

"Maybe, but I wasn't really counting. Orgasms or minutes."

"Me neither," I admitted, wrapping an arm around her, pulling her even closer to me.

Stay, Simone.

I found a familiar phrase echoing in my mind, even though I knew she'd probably be heading for the door any moment now. She didn't seem exceptionally tired, which meant that she'd have enough energy to get up and go back to her own bed for the night.

"How much would it cost to put in bookshelves?"

"What?" Her question caught me off guard.

"In my bedroom," she explained. "There are already bookshelves in there, but I meant the ones that are actually built into the wall? I was watching a video online with a woman who had them and they looked so chic."

"Are you thinking about making some adjustments to your room?"

"Nothing that would bring down your home's valuation." She chuckled. "Don't worry. I'll also make sure it's stuff you can take out without too much trouble."

"I don't care if you bring down my home's valuation. I

don't care if you decide to paint your entire room lime green."

"Be careful what you wish for." Simone chuckled again. "Because I'm pretty sure lime green is literally always on sale at the paint store."

Simone looked up at me and kissed me on the chin. Then she settled back down next to me, letting out a small sigh.

"I could get used to this," she murmured.

"Me too," I murmured back, hoping against hope that we were talking about the same thing. I gingerly ran a hand through her hair as sleep slowly crept in, my eyes soon closing as I let myself sink off to sleep.

But as I nodded off, all I could think about was how good it felt to hold Simone in my arms like this.

And how much it was going to hurt when I couldn't hold her anymore.

31

SIMONE

I woke up in Harry's arms.

I smiled to myself at the realization, his breath coming slow and steady as he still slept beside me—

"Crap!" I suddenly yelled after my brain fully came back online. I had a doctor's appointment this morning, and I had no idea what time it was. I'd set an alarm in my room last night, but since I hadn't slept in my room, that alarm might as well have been in another country.

I frantically hopped out of bed, running toward Harry's bedroom door.

"Simone? Are you okay? Where are you going?" Harry called out after me.

"Doctor's appointment! I'm late!"

"Why are you going to the doctor?" he asked, but I was already too far away to answer without screaming back at him. I stumbled into my bedroom, heading right for the closet. I hastily put together an outfit, pulling different tops and pants off their hangers. When I was satisfied with a black-and-white dress, I pulled it over my head and shook out my hair.

Wait.

Should I take a shower?

I pulled my dress off as I hurried into the bathroom to take a quick shower. It didn't take me long to dry off and get back into the dress, my heart pounding against my chest with my every move. It felt like I was playing a dangerous game, running late for an OB/GYN appointment when me being pregnant in the first place was pretty much a miracle.

Mom.

Crap!

I ran to Mom's rehab room, making sure she was in for her session today. My mom didn't even notice that I'd come into the room as she worked with one of the nurses Harry had hired to help her do her rehab at home.

"There you go, Miss Eileen. Just like that." The nurse was smiling down at her. "We're going to start off slow, okay? We don't need to rush through this. It's more important that you're all the way healed. That's the most important thing, okay?"

I offered them a quick wave, but neither of them seemed to notice that I existed.

Good.

I was running late, anyway. I didn't have time to make small talk with the nurse, and I could always catch up with my mom later.

I ran outside the house, and a few moments later, I was sitting in the back of a cab and heading to Dr. Carlson's office. I checked my phone as I held a breath, realizing that I was already ten minutes late.

Didn't Dr. Carlson's office consider appointments a no-show if they were fifteen minutes late?

When I finally arrived at her office, I rushed through the doors, only stopping when I bumped into the front desk.

"Appointment! I have an appointment! Dr. Carlson. At 9:15 a.m."

"Of course." The woman behind the desk gave me a wide smile. "Mrs. O'Donnell, yes? Your husband already checked in for the both of you. He's waiting for you in room three."

My husband?

"My husband?" I repeated the thought out loud. "My husband's here?"

"Is there a problem?" The woman's face fell. Her eyes went wide, and she lowered her voice. "Do you feel unsafe with him, ma'am? If you're not safe, we have options for you—"

"No! No." I shook my head. "It's fine. I just wasn't expecting him to come to this appointment. He's usually too busy to make these things."

"Well, it looks like he's making time for you today." She beamed. "Have a good day, Mrs. O'Donnell."

"You, too." I headed toward the back of the doctor's office, my stomach feeling like it was stuck in my throat.

A part of me was hoping that the woman at the front desk was mistaken, that once I walked through the exam room door, there'd be a different man waiting there–some guy who'd made a mistake and wandered into the wrong room.

But of course, as soon as I pushed open the door, Harry was right there, sitting in one of the guest chairs.

Double crap.

"What are you doing here, Harry?" I asked as I took a seat beside him. "Did you follow me here or something?"

"I don't have to follow you anywhere, Simone. I run one of the biggest magazines in the country." He scoffed. "I have investigative journalists I can call at the drop of a hat."

"And what? They were able to figure out where I was going? In, like, less than five minutes?"

"I think it took them around ten, but I had a head start by already being in the car. I just needed to know where to go," he replied. "Although, I feel like the better question is what are *you* doing here, Simone?"

"Are you saying I can't go to the doctor without permission?"

"No. I'm saying it's weird that you didn't tell me about it."

"Sorry? But I didn't think I needed to tell you about what I'm doing every minute of the day."

"Are you sick?" he pressed, concern lining his voice. "Were you hiding it because you thought we needed to focus on your mom? Because I don't have a problem with multitasking, Simone, and if you're sick, you need to tell me—"

"I'm not sick, Harry."

"Oh." He softened as he relaxed into his chair. "Is this just for a routine appointment, then? Because if that's the case, you're right. I don't need to be here. And I definitely owe you an apology for freaking out over nothing—"

"I'm not here for a routine appointment, either." My eyes welled with tears as I looked over at Harry. I knew that I should've told him the truth so much earlier, and now, I had no idea how he was going to respond.

And I was terrified of losing him.

"Simone?" Harry's voice was low. "Is everything all right?"

"I'm pregnant."

He blinked at me. "You... what?"

"I'm pregnant, Harry," I repeated, tears streaming down my face. "I'm sorry. I'm so sorry. I should've told you so much sooner—"

"Is it mine?"

"Harry, what are you talking about?" My sadness quickly shifted into anger. "Are you seriously asking me that right now?"

"I'm not—I didn't mean—" Harry seemed flustered. "I'm sorry. I was just thinking that Jace sent you that thing about fertility. I know you didn't reply to him, and I know you don't want to be with him, but I don't know if you decided to go through with a sperm donor or what you were thinking—"

"A sperm donor?" I narrowed my eyes at him. "Yeah, I used a sperm donor, Harry. I'm looking right at him."

"But I thought you couldn't—I thought that we couldn't—" Harry blinked fast. "I'm just confused. This whole time, you told me that you couldn't get pregnant. I even asked you if we needed to use protection—"

"That's because I thought we didn't. The fact that I'm pregnant is pretty much a miracle," I said, before placing my palm on his thigh. "I'm sorry, okay? I should've told you as soon as I knew, but I didn't know how you'd react. I know that you don't want kids—"

Harry stared at me for a long moment, something changing in his face. Finally, he spoke in a cold tone.

"Did you *plan* this, Simone?"

My jaw dropped. "What's that supposed to mean, Harry?"

"I think you know exactly what it means, Simone." Harry's eyes had turned chilly. "Why else would you let any of this happen if it wasn't what you wanted? Why would you ever let yourself get pregnant if you really thought we were going to get divorced in a few months?"

"Harry—"

"Has any of this even been real?" Harry murmured. "Is

this all you wanted from the beginning? You just wanted to secure a place in my family? You just wanted to make sure you could have access to me and my family's money?"

"You should choose your next words very carefully, Harry O'Donnell," I warned. "Because if you're about to accuse me of being a gold digger—"

"Aren't you?"

I went quiet at the accusation, my heart breaking into pieces inside my chest.

Just then, Dr. Carlson stepped into the room. "Simone. It's nice to see you again, as always. And this must be Harry?"

She reached out to shake Harry's hand, and he returned the gesture, his face blank.

"The front desk told me you checked in with Simone today. It's so nice to finally meet you."

Harry didn't say anything in response. Dr. Carlson seemed to tense up at that, and she looked back over at me.

"Come on. Let's get you up on the exam table. I need to get the ultrasound all set up."

I glanced at Harry, suddenly sick to my stomach.

32

SIMONE

"Everything looks as expected," Dr. Carlson said as she moved the ultrasound wand around my abdomen. "No surprises, which is always a good thing."

Harry was still sitting in the corner of the room, his eyes burning a hole through the back of my head. It was almost like I could read his thoughts, like I could feel how much he resented me at that moment. I was doing my very best to ignore the rage rolling off him, and I had a feeling that Dr. Carlson was doing the same.

Poor Dr. Carlson.

This was the second time I'd put her in an awkward professional situation with the man I was dating—

Wait.

Were Harry and I even together anymore?

And if we weren't ever *really* together, could we even have a real breakup?

"So, everything looks okay?" I asked, trying to take my focus off the thoughts running through my mind.

Dr. Carlson hummed. "I'm a little worried about the

adhesions I'm seeing in your womb, but we always knew those might be a problem. The baby's implanted well, but the adhesions could affect its ability to grow throughout the rest of your pregnancy."

"Is there anything I can do about it?" I was hopeful, despite the fact that part of me feared the worst.

"The best thing you can do in this scenario is take it easy," she answered. "In fact, I'm going to recommend you go on bed rest for part of your pregnancy."

"Bed rest?"

"Yes, the sooner the better, really. I just don't think we should take any chances here. You already know the odds aren't exactly with us on this one. We're quite literally trying to deliver a miracle."

"Right. A miracle." I nodded, then turned to look over at Harry, who was still stewing in the corner.

A miracle that only one of us wants or believes in.

I fought the urge to cry as I finished up my appointment with Dr. Carlson. And when it was time to check out of her office, I headed out to the lobby on my own.

Not knowing or caring if Harry was behind me.

～

"Simone? Are you seriously trying to ignore me?" Harry caught up with me as I walked outside of the doctor's office.

"I'm not ignoring you. I just don't feel like talking to you right now."

"I don't think you get to pull that card. Not after what you just told me back there." Harry was suddenly in front of me, blocking my path. "I just don't understand. If you were pregnant with my baby, why wouldn't you just tell me? Why'd you keep it a secret from me?"

"I already told you, Harry. I didn't know how you were going to react—" I threw up my hands in pure exasperation. "And you know what? I was right not to tell you!"

"How could you say something like that?"

"Uh, maybe because you called me a gold digger?" I let out a frustrated laugh. "Or did you forget that you just accused me of planning this whole thing to scheme my way into your family and wealth?"

"You know I didn't mean that, Simone. I was just pissed—"

"It sounded like you meant it to me, Harry."

"Fine. Maybe I meant some of it," he admitted. "But could you blame me? You're being so shady about this whole thing—"

"I'm moving out."

"What?"

"I'm moving out, Harry. I'm gone." I held up my hands as I spoke. "I don't need this energy right now, okay? You heard the doctor. I can't take any chances and that includes living with someone who's going to stress me out all the time."

"Simone—"

"Don't. Don't try to convince me to stay after you just called me a gold digger." I shook my head. "Trust me. If I'm as bad of a person as you think I am, then you should be happy to have me gone. Right?"

"Simone, don't—"

"I've got to go. I've got a cab to catch." I stepped around Harry as I continued walking down the street. I secretly hoped that he wouldn't try to chase after me, that he wouldn't try to block my path again.

Because if he did, he would've seen how hard I was crying.

He would've seen how much he'd hurt me, and I couldn't let him know how easy it was for him to completely shatter me, how easy it was for him to break me into pieces.

33

HARRY

"Seriously? You're pulling this trick again?" Simone groaned as soon as she walked through the door of the house. "How did you even beat me back home this time?"

I was fuming while waiting for Simone to get back home, everything in me feeling like it was hot enough to set off flames.

How the hell could she have kept something so big from me?

How could she not tell me that she was pregnant with my child?

It was the kind of betrayal that I could've never seen coming. At least, not from Simone.

Because I'd never expected Simone to ever betray me like this. Ever.

"Simple. I didn't have to catch a cab." I answered her question as I held up a pair of car keys before setting them down on a nearby table. "I would've offered you a ride if you weren't so committed to stomping away from our conversation—"

"Because we don't have anything else to talk about."

"I disagree."

"Why? Because you feel like yelling at me? You want to tell me again how mad at me you are?"

"I'm just trying to understand what happened here." I sighed before I nodded toward the hall. "Do you mind talking somewhere more private? Maybe my home office? I don't want your mom or the nurse to accidentally overhear—"

"Sure. Whatever." Simone brushed past me, her demeanor completely cold. I followed behind her until we reached my home office, and once we were both inside, I quietly closed the door behind us.

"You don't need to leave," I started. "It wouldn't make any sense if you did."

"Because?"

"Because the doctor wants you to be on bed rest soon. And because your mom is still recovering from her surgery," I replied. "How are you going to take care of her when you need to be taken care of yourself? Besides, your apartment is way too small for her to do her rehab stuff, anyway."

"Why do you care? If I'm such a bad person, why does it matter what happens to me and my mom?"

"I care because you're having a child with me, Simone. And I'm going to be there for my child, no matter what happens with us."

"I don't know. I think it's better if we make a clean break." She shrugged. "I don't want to feel like I owe you anything."

"This isn't just about you, Simone. We're having a kid together now."

I hated this.

I hated arguing with Simone like this. I hated that we ever got to this point.

Even though I was pissed at Simone, some part of me wanted to try to move past this. Hell, I kind of liked the idea of coparenting with Simone... because I liked the idea of doing *anything* with Simone. Even things I wasn't sure I was ready for.

Still, I couldn't deny I was angry about how all this went down.

"You're pretty quiet," Simone said as she studied me. "Something on your mind?"

"Trust me. You don't want to know."

"Is it about how I'm a no-good gold digger who sank her claws into your family's fortune?"

"I don't know."

Simone scoffed. "Seriously, Harry? You really think that little of me?"

"I don't even think you did it on purpose, Simone. I think you saw how different our lives were, and you just—"

"Decided that I was going to scam you by getting myself pregnant?"

"I think you decided that you'd rather be comfortable than struggle, and on the surface, there's nothing wrong with that," I replied. "Hell, maybe you were just looking out for your mom—"

"Nope," Simone cut me off. "I can't stay here, Harry. Not if that's what you seriously think of me after all this time. You really think that I'd do that to you?"

"Simone—"

"I can be out in a week. My mom and I will figure things out on our own."

"Stop." I gently grabbed her hand. "Don't make decisions when you're upset like this—"

Simone pulled her hand away from me, her eyes on me

like I was a complete stranger. "You don't get to tell me how to feel, Harry."

Fuck.

I could feel something shifting between us and it hurt.

"Fine." I walked out of the office and glanced at her from the hallway. "If one of us can't be here anymore, then it's going to be me."

"Wait. What? But this is your house!" Simone trailed behind me as I headed toward my bedroom. "You're really going to move out of your own place?"

"Eileen needs to get better, and you need to start making plans for bed rest," I said. I entered my bedroom and pulled a suitcase out of the closet. "I can always make reservations at the Waldorf for the rest of the week. Maybe longer."

"Harry—"

"You don't get to tell me what to do, Simone," I said, echoing her words from earlier. "You should probably go check on your mom. We can catch up later. Or not."

"Or not." Simone nodded before she left my bedroom. I waited to see if she would've at least turned to look at me, just one last time.

But she never looked back. Not even once.

And I felt the gap between us growing even wider.

~

"Harry. There you are." My mom greeted me with a warm smile as I walked through the entryway of my parents' house later that day. "You look as handsome as ever."

"Thanks, Mom." I faked a smile as she pulled me in for a hug.

I was all dressed up in a suit and tie, at my mom's

request. Today was the day they were signing the company over to me, and apparently, it was tradition to hire a photographer for the occasion. Which meant that I needed to look my best or else I risked embarrassing the family name.

"There you are, son." My dad appeared in the foyer with a huge grin on his face. "You look great. Did Simone help you pick out your outfit?"

"Something like that, yeah."

More like she hasn't spoken to me in a day.

Not a text. Not a phone call.

Not even an email just to check in.

"I'm not surprised." My mom chuckled. "Simone seems like someone who knows how to present herself. Of course, she'd want her husband to look good, too."

"Speaking of, your brother wanted to know if Simone is planning anything for your birthday? It's right around the corner, you know, and Sean wants to be included if she is planning something. He's very excited about it."

"Ruby seems excited, too. I think both of them are quite smitten with Simone—"

"Can we not talk about Simone right now?" I accidentally raised my voice, quickly bringing it back down to a normal tone. "It's just—today isn't about my marriage. Today is about the family business and securing its future."

"Of course, Harry. Of course." My mom softly patted me on the shoulder. "We can save the Simone talk for another time."

I watched as she exchanged a glance with my father, both of them seeming concerned.

"We're fine. Everything's fine," I lied. "Sorry. I've just been under a lot of stress lately. I didn't mean to take it out on either of you."

"These things happen," Dad reassured me. "And even if

there is something going on between you and Simone, I know how smart you both are. You'll figure it out, all in due time."

"Until then, let's get that photo snapped, yes?" Mom beamed before she motioned for me to follow behind her. I did as I was told, even though my mind was somewhere else.

"Don't lose her," my dad whispered, so low that I almost didn't hear him say anything.

"What?"

"Don't lose her." This time, my dad looked at me as he spoke. "That's my advice. If you love her, don't let her go. You might think that you can just replace people, that there'll always be someone out there for you. But the truth of it, son? Sometimes, if you're lucky, you only get the one. You don't need to find anyone else when the right person for you is already in your life."

"Thanks, Dad. I'll try my best." My tone was dismissive. "We'll see what happens."

"I'm not saying this to be cruel, son," he continued. "And I understand things don't always work out, even when we try our best. I just want you to be happy, and sometimes, happiness is something we have to fight for."

I just want you to be happy.

The words sank into my skin as we moved into position to pose for the picture. I sat at a table holding a pen in my hand, pretending to sign the document in front of me, with my parents standing on either side of me.

Was that true?

Was that all my parents really wanted for me?

My dad hadn't mentioned the business once, or what would happen if Simone and I got divorced too soon. It was almost like it wasn't part of his calculations anymore, like he genuinely cared more about our relationship than the future of *LA Now*.

Maybe Simone had been right.

Maybe I didn't need to completely shut my parents out or pull away from them so much. Maybe there was something we could salvage, somewhere down the line.

As a family.

My hotel room was lonely.

At first, I figured there was too much space for one person–the suite was more like an apartment with its full kitchen, living room, and private terrace.

Then it hit me. The suite felt too big because someone was missing.

Because I was missing Simone.

Shit.

I'd fucked up everything, hadn't I?

Why the hell was I accusing Simone of being a gold digger? It was obvious that she didn't care about my money. She'd never even asked me about how much money I had. She seemed to have no interest in learning the specifics of it.

Was it just a defense mechanism? Was I trying to protect myself from getting hurt by pushing her away with the worst kind of accusation?

I couldn't pretend I wasn't terrified of how things were going to change between us. Even if Simone and I decided to be in a real relationship now, how long would it last before things fizzled out? How much longer until it stopped being about her and me, and more about our family?

We'd barely have any time together before we had to be parents.

Assuming that Simone still wanted to be with me at all.

I groaned as I fell back against my bed, my head suddenly thrumming with pain and regret.

Would Simone even want to try with me? Could she forgive me after all the bullshit I'd said to her? That I'd accused her of?

I couldn't shake the feeling that it was already too late for us. That no matter what I said or did now, Simone had already made up her mind.

There was a crushing weight on my chest, swirling into the pain that still throbbed in my head.

I'd lost everything.

Simone. Our future together. Our baby.

I'd lost everything because I was too afraid to have it.

And I was going to hate myself for the rest of my life for it.

34

SIMONE

I didn't miss Harry.

That was what I kept telling myself, even if there was a hole in my heart.

It was so much harder being away from him than I could've ever imagined. Even though we hadn't been together that long, he'd clearly had an effect on every part of me. It didn't help that I was still living in his house, haunted with memories of him in every corner.

Still, I'd need to find a way to get over him, sooner rather than later.

After he'd accused me of being after his money and left, I realized that we never truly knew each other. There was no way he could've really gotten to know me and accuse me of something like that, which made me wonder if everything between us had something shallow at the center.

Maybe we just liked each other in bed. And I'd made the mistake of thinking there was something more to it than there was.

"Is Harry still at work?" Mom asked as she turned the

corner into the kitchen in her wheelchair. "It's been two days since I've seen him, hasn't it?"

"It's a really busy time," I replied with a forced smile. "I'm not surprised if he's been sleeping at the office. When it gets chaotic like that, they need all hands on deck."

"Are you sure about that?"

"Sure about Harry being busy?"

"Are you sure that you want to lie to me about this, Simi?" she answered. "Instead of just telling me the truth?"

"How do you know I'm lying to you?"

"Because I can read you like a book." My mom sighed. "And because even if Harry was spending his nights at the office, there'd still be some kind of sign of life from him. He seems like the type who'd send you flowers and a singing telegram if he was away from you for more than a few hours."

"A singing telegram?" I playfully scoffed. "I don't think either of us would enjoy that very much."

"I'm serious, Simi. What's going on?"

"What's going on is that you're going to be a grandmother."

"Wait. Really?" My mom's eyes went wide.

"Yes, really." I smiled down at her, this time the expression genuine. "I would've told you sooner, but I didn't want to distract you from your surgery. I wanted you to focus all your energy on your recovery."

"Are you sure?" Mom reached out to grab my hand.

"Sure about what?"

"Sure about the baby," she nearly whispered. "I don't want you to get your hopes up, Simi. I remember how it was with Jace. If something happens to the baby—"

"I think it's going to be okay this time, Mom," I said with

tears in my eyes. "I'll need to be on bed rest pretty soon, just to be on the safe side. But yeah. I think I'm actually going to be a mom. It's finally happening for me."

"And it's happening with the man you love." She squeezed my hand in her palm. "This is such a beautiful moment, Simone. I'm so happy for you."

I felt myself start to cry, hard, before I had a chance to catch myself.

"Oh, Simi. What's wrong?"

"You were right, about Harry being gone. He's not sleeping at his office. He's sleeping in a hotel room."

"Why? What happened?"

"We had a big fight." I sniffled. "We both said things that we regret, or at least, I hope he regrets what he said, too."

"What were you fighting about?"

I took a moment to think over the question. I didn't want to tell my mom everything Harry said, because I didn't want her to think any less of him. And there was no way she wouldn't be as furious as I was if I told her about the gold digger accusations. She'd probably try to have us moved out of Harry's house by the end of the day.

Ugh.

Even when I was upset with him, I still wanted to protect him.

I still wanted to protect the idea of *us*.

"We were fighting about the baby," I finally answered. "Harry thought that I couldn't get pregnant. The same thing I thought, too. And he wasn't really ready for it when I told him that we're having a child together."

"Oh." My mom's face fell. "Well, that's a little upsetting. And disappointing."

"You can't blame him." I quickly shook my head.

"Having a kid is a really big deal and he never even thought it was in the cards for him. It's a lot to adjust to."

"Still. To leave you here alone?"

"We both need time to figure out how we feel, Mom. That's all this is." I squeezed her hand back. "And I'm not alone, am I? I'm pretty sure you're here with me, unless this is just a hallucination I'm having."

"Hmm." My mom thought for a moment, then looked at me. "I guess even good husbands make mistakes sometimes. No one's perfect, and if you're sure that he's coming back, then I guess we'll just have to wait for him to come home."

"He will. He'll come home soon."

"Of course, he will, Simi." My mom smiled. "Now, let's think about what we want for lunch. I'm absolutely starving."

As my mom rolled past me to open the fridge, I felt something sink inside my chest.

He'll come home.

It was one of the biggest lies I'd ever told. I had no idea if Harry was ever going to come home. At least not to *me*. And if he did, there was no guarantee it was going to be a happy reunion.

For all I knew, he was coming home to break my heart.

~

Later that night, I was falling to pieces.

I still hadn't heard anything from Harry, and it was starting to feel like maybe I never would again. I'd checked my phone so many times that my eyes were about to cross from staring at the screen, but I couldn't help myself.

Could he really just pretend like I never existed?

I curled up against my mattress as thoughts ran through my head.

Of course, he could pretend like I never existed. He had enough money to erase me from his personal history, enough money to bury our marriage if he wanted to.

But did he want to?

He clearly didn't want to have a child with me. And if he didn't want a child with me, that meant that he didn't really want to be part of our child's life, either.

Or part of mine.

It didn't matter that he was going to let my mom and me stay here throughout her recovery or throughout my pregnancy. That was him being kind enough to not be a complete asshole, but it didn't mean that he was going to keep tabs on me once we were all moved out.

Outside of maybe sending money to make sure our kid wasn't starving.

I closed my eyes as a painful image flashed in my brain, one where Harry was married to someone else in the future, where he had the family that he actually asked for, a beautiful woman on his arm and their children posed with them around their home.

He was the happiest he'd ever been. And I was just a distant memory.

God.

What if I accidentally ran into them in the street? Harry's old life crashing right into his new one. Would he even acknowledge us as his old family?

I knew that I was never going to fall in love again, because I couldn't handle getting hurt like this again. A person could only survive this kind of heartbreak so many times before she became completely hollow.

And I couldn't be hollow. I needed to be strong for the

baby growing inside of me. I needed to still be able to love and be loved, to experience warmth and joy and happiness. Even if Harry had the power to break me, I could never break.

Even if right now, I felt more broken than ever.

35

HARRY

"Harry? Are you in there?" My mother's voice was on the other side of my hotel room door. "Harry!"

I cracked open an eye as I looked over at the door. I was surprised to hear my mom's voice, especially considering that I hadn't told her I was staying here.

"Harry! If you don't let us in, we'll get security from the lobby to do it!" My dad's voice was coming through the door now, too. "Don't make us turn this into a whole thing, son. Just open the door."

I rolled out of bed, still confused by my parents showing up. I pulled open the door and saw concerned looks on both of their faces.

"Oh my God. We were so worried about you!" My mom pulled me in for a tight hug. "Don't ever do that to us again!"

"What did I do to you?" I asked as I saw my father shaking his head out of the corner of my eye.

"Don't pretend like you don't know what you've done, son. You haven't answered our calls in days."

"Days?" I murmured. "It's been days?"

I grimaced as the realization hit me. I hadn't been keeping track of much of anything outside of work calls, work meetings and anything involving the magazine. In fact, I'd been so hyper-focused on work that everything else had fallen by the wayside. And when I wasn't working, I spent the majority of my free time trying to avoid things that reminded me of Simone or anything that made me think of her.

Which meant that I'd been pretty much lost to the world, apparently for *days*.

"Sorry. I've just been working." I shrugged. "Someone has to keep the lights on at *LA Now*, right?"

"Oh, please." My mom rolled her eyes. "It's more than working too much, Harry."

"No, I'm pretty sure it was just work—"

"I know how you think about us," my mom cut me off. "I know that we were hard on you growing up, you and your brother. And I know that we asked too much of you. We made you feel like you had to be perfect. And I always knew that you liked to keep your distance from us, Harry, but—"

My mom got all choked up before she went on. "I hope you know how much we care about you, even if we haven't done our best. We were trying. We really were. We may have made some mistakes, but please, don't punish us for them. Not forever."

"We want to be part of your life, son," my dad added. "That's all we've ever wanted. Please. Don't lock us out."

"Lock you out?" I held up my hands in defense. "I'm not trying to lock anyone out. Like I said, I've just been busy."

"We talked to Paul. He said you haven't come into work in a week, that you've insisted on working from home?"

Mom said, her eyes locked on mine. "That's not usual for you, Harry. It sounds like you're avoiding something."

"Oh my God. It's like I'm talking to a wall." I groaned in pure frustration as I took a seat on the edge of my hotel bed. "Nothing's wrong. I'm fine. Sorry for missing your calls. I'll check my phone more often."

"If you're fine, then where's your wife?" Mom pressed. "Does she even know where you are? Or does she think you've been sleeping at the office?"

"Simone's not my wife."

"What?" My dad rushed toward me. "You two are splitting up?"

"We never were really a couple," I admitted. "Simone and I only got married so I could get the company."

"Harry!" Mom gasped. "Are you serious?"

"I am. I'd only met her a day or two before I asked her to sign a contract and agree to marry me. She was a new hire at my company and we clicked. We clicked so much that I thought it'd be enough to convince other people that there was something real between us."

"Why would you do something like that?" My dad scrunched up his face in confusion. "I don't understand. So, you were lying to me that day in your office? When you said you already had someone in mind to marry?"

"Yes." I shrugged. "Because you told me it was the only way to keep my position as CEO. I was willing to do whatever it took to run *LA Now* because I'm good at it. Because I love my job. And the thought of you handing it over to Sean just because he had Ruby?"

I let out a harsh laugh. "You told me that I was going to lose everything I cared about, and you're seriously surprised that I was willing to fight for it?"

"You were never going to lose *LA Now*." My dad sighed, then took a seat next to me on the bed.

I blinked. "What?"

"It was always an empty threat," he admitted. "We knew that you were the best choice to run *LA Now*. Your mother and I were just getting concerned about you. We knew that you weren't spending time on your personal life, and we were worried that one day, you'd regret it. That you'd look around and have no one."

"I would've had a successful company. That would've been enough for me." I sank my head into my hands. "None of this had to happen. If you hadn't insisted on me being married by my fortieth birthday, maybe I could've taken things slow with Simone. Maybe we could've had a shot at something real."

"I'm sorry." My dad placed a comforting hand on my back. "You're right. We shouldn't have tried to control what you did with your life. That wasn't fair for us to do. We just wanted you to give love a chance, but it sounds like we should've just waited. Simone was already on her way to you."

"And I'm so happy she found her way to you, son." My mom sat on the other side of me. "Still. Did something happen between you two? Even if your marriage is fake, why wouldn't she be here with you? Why are you two not together right now?"

"Because I messed everything up."

"What happened?"

"Simone's pregnant," I answered, my head still in my hands. "And instead of being there for her, I decided to accuse her of being a gold digger who was trying to scheme her way into our family."

"You did what?" My mom gasped again. "Harry! That's the worst thing you could've said to her!"

"I know."

"You're lucky if she talks to you ever again!"

"I know, I know." I sighed. "I was the one who told you that I messed everything up, remember? I know how bad this is."

"I think you could still fix it." Dad patted me on the back. "It might take some elbow grease and a whole lot of luck, but anything's possible if you two love each other."

"That's the thing. I don't even know if she loves me. I don't know how she really feels about me, and after the whole gold digger thing, I imagine she's not in the mood to have a conversation about how we feel about each other."

"You'll figure something out, Harry. I know you will." Mom patted my back now, too. "Besides, only a fool would let someone like Simone get away from them. And the one thing you've never been is a fool, son. Not a day in your life."

"Thanks, Mom." I blew out a heavy breath as my parents continued to comfort me with their presence. It was a new feeling for me, leaning on them in a time of need. But it was new for them to seem so concerned about my well-being and my life, too. Strangely, in the middle of what was one of the worst things I'd ever been through, it felt like I was turning over a new leaf in my relationship with my parents.

Like there was going to actually be a way forward for us.

Like we were actually going to be a real family for what felt like the first time in forever.

I just hoped the same was possible with Simone.

∽

"My birthday party."

"What?" Mom was staring at a piece of art hanging in the hallway, her attention seemingly broken by me speaking to her. I'd been spending the last two days at my parents' home, enjoying the time spent around my family, too.

It definitely beat being holed up in a hotel room, slowly losing all sense of the passing of time.

"I need you to invite Simone to my birthday party," I said. "It can't come from me, or else she's either going to ignore it or she won't show up."

"Why do you think me asking her would make any difference?" My mom was puzzled by the request. "If she's avoiding you, isn't she avoiding all of us?"

"She likes you. And she wouldn't want to be rude. If you invited her somewhere, she'd show up, only if it was for a few minutes."

"So, you want me to invite your wife to your birthday party in the hopes that she stays for *a few minutes*?"

"Yep!"

"Harry?"

"Yeah?"

"What exactly are you planning?" Mom pressed. "Besides your own birthday party, apparently."

"You'll see."

"Oh. I'm sure." My mom pulled out her phone, then casually dialed a number. "Eileen! There you are! I haven't heard from you in so long! Sorry it's been a while since I called. How is your therapy going?"

Eileen?

My mom called Eileen to talk to her regularly?

I opened my mouth to say something, but quickly

decided to close it instead. There had to be a method to my mother's madness, and a part of me wanted to wait and see how the whole thing played out.

"That sounds awful, but also amazing. I'm happy to hear that the prospects are so good long-term," my mom continued. "Listen, Eileen. I'm sure you know this by now, but it looks like Harry has made a complete mess of things with Simone and he'd like to try to make them better."

My throat closed as I waited.

"His plan? To invite her to his birthday party." Mom looked at me as she spoke. "No, I know. I'm sure there's more to it than that. But here's the thing. He needs to make sure that Simone actually shows up. Do you think you could convince her to come? Maybe as a favor to her dear mother?"

My mother suddenly held up a finger. "Hold on. Let me ask him."

She moved the phone away from her mouth, then said, "Eileen wants to know if you're serious about this. If you are, she says she can get Simone to show up. But she doesn't want her daughter showing up just to get her heart broken."

I nodded. "I'm serious about this. Dead serious."

"Great." Mom moved the phone back up to her mouth. "He says he's dead serious, Eileen, and I believe him. What do you say? Do we have a deal?"

A few seconds passed before my mom was smiling wide. "Of course. We'll see you both on Saturday. I'll let Harry send over the details."

"That's it? She's coming?" Hope welled up within me. "She's really coming?"

"So says Eileen."

"Yes!" I pumped the air with my fist, losing myself in a

moment of excitement. "Shit! I've got so much to figure out by Saturday!"

"Language, Harry." Mom smirked. "But yes, it does sound like you have quite a lot of work to do. You should get on that."

"I will!" I practically took off running down the hall. I had to come up with something worthy of Simone.

Something that would finally make her want to stay.

36

SIMONE

*B*eing pregnant was the *worst*.
But also the *best*?

Everything was so confusing. My emotions. My physical state.

It didn't help that I was seemingly nauseous all the time now, no matter what. I seemed to be one of the unlucky women who were woozy their entire first trimester.

Still, even with all the nausea, I wouldn't have traded being pregnant for anything in the world—

Wait. What day was it?

I'd been mostly spending my days going from my bed to the bathroom, with a few trips to the kitchen fridge thrown in for good measure. And since I was still reeling from my relationship with Harry ending in disaster, I'd been trying my best to stop thinking about him. Which meant that I'd filled my days with conversations with Taylor, conversations with my mom, conversations with anyone who'd talk to me about anything other than Harry O'Donnell.

Unfortunately, with each passing day, I was starting to

worry that getting over him wasn't actually possible, no matter how much I avoided talking about him.

Ugh.

I pulled up the calendar on my phone, wanting to distract myself from thoughts of Harry, as I made my way to the kitchen. Even if I didn't have anywhere to be anytime soon, it was probably still good to know what day it was, just in general.

Of course, by trying to avoid Harry, I ran into another reminder of him.

It was Saturday. *Harry's birthday.*

If things were better between us, we probably would've gone out to celebrate at some fancy restaurant. We would've been trying each other's pasta as Harry asked the server which wine he recommended with his dish, and the best dessert that would've paired with it, too. I would've cracked a few jokes about him taking his food way too seriously. He would've rolled his eyes before he called me beautiful.

And we would've come back home to spend the night together, getting lost in Harry's bedsheets as he reminded me, again and again, that I was his and only his.

My heart broke at the thought of it. It would've been magical, being like that again.

Just being us.

I shook my head as I reached for an apple on the kitchen counter. There was no point in living in a fantasyland. I needed to focus on taking care of the baby and taking care of me.

I needed to focus on what was real.

"Simi?"

I jumped at the sound of my mom's voice. "Mom! You scared me." I squinted as I looked over at her. "Why are you dressed up right now?"

"We have somewhere to be today, don't we?"

"No?" I finally took a bite of my apple, enjoying its crisp texture. "It's Saturday, so I know we don't have a doctor's appointment. And you look overdressed for the doctor's office, anyway."

I took a moment to appreciate my mom's outfit. She was wearing a purple dress with a matching shawl, the look complete with a set of pearls around her neck.

"Did your nurse help you get dressed?"

"Yes, but some of it I was able to do on my own." She smiled. "I'm getting better, even if it's only a little bit at a time."

"That's good to hear, Mom." I smiled back at her. "But I still don't know where we're supposed to be going, so you're going to have to fill me in."

"We're going to Harry's birthday party."

"Nope. No, thanks!" I chuckled, taking another bite of my apple. "But if you want to go, I don't mind dropping you off. You can just tell his family that I said hey—"

"We're going, Simi," Mom pressed. "You need to get dressed so we can head over."

"But we're not talking to each other right now."

"I don't care. Grace invited us. It'd be rude not to show up."

"But what if he doesn't want me there?" I frowned. "I don't think I could handle being kicked out of my own husband's birthday party. The embarrassment would be enough to kill me."

"Simi—"

"And what if I don't feel like socializing? You know how nauseous I've been with the pregnancy. It's probably safer for me if I stay close to a bathroom. You don't want me throwing up all over Grace, now, do you—"

"Simone, go to your room and get dressed." She shook her head. "I'm not going to talk to you about this anymore. The decision has already been made."

It was no use arguing with her. She wasn't taking no for an answer.

And she was right. I couldn't hide from him forever.

"I can't believe this is happening to me right now," I murmured as I went back to my bedroom. I hopped into the shower, just for a quick rinse, then stood in front of my closet.

Harry's birthday party.

What the hell was I supposed to wear? I didn't want to dress too flirty, because he might think that meant I was already looking for the next guy to date. And I didn't want to dress like I wasn't trying to flirt, at all, because then he might think that I didn't want him to even try to make a move.

"Simi! Hurry up, or we're going to be late!"

"I'm coming!" I huffed out a breath before I pulled on a classy pale pink dress with embroidered sleeves. It was sleek and formfitting, but there wasn't any cleavage and the hem of it nearly brushed against the floor.

Perfect.

"Whoa. What happened to the coffee shop?"

I was stunned as I stepped through its doors. The place had been completely transformed into some kind of wonderland. The usual overhead lights were turned completely off, with sparkling fairy lights hanging off vines all across the ceiling instead. Each table in the coffee shop had mugs on top of them, too, each one filled with scented candles that made the entire room smell like vanilla and cream.

"This is gorgeous," Mom murmured by my side. "Have you ever been here before, Simone?"

My eyes welled with tears. "Yeah, Mom. This is where I met Harry for the first time."

"Oh." Her voice went quiet.

"I don't think I can do this, Mom." I wiped a tear away from my face. "I'm sorry. I'm just going to head back to the car. You can tell everyone I came, but I started feeling too sick to stay. Being here hurts way too much—"

"Simone?" Harry's voice suddenly cut through my words.

I turned around to see him walking toward me. He was dressed in an expensive-looking suit, with an even more expensive-looking watch on his wrist.

He looked just like he did on the first day we met. Like he was too busy for anything outside himself.

Like he was too busy for someone like me.

"What is this, Harry?" My voice was low. "Why are you doing this?"

"Why am I doing what? Having a birthday party?"

"This is torture." I sniffled. "You have to realize that, right? If you were trying to be the winner in this breakup, then congratulations. You won."

"Simone—" Harry took a step closer to me. "Baby."

Baby?

Before Harry could say another word, I watched as the rest of his family appeared behind him. All of them looked so nervous, yet they also seemed cautious, like they were waiting on some kind of cue. His mom looked particularly anxious, even though she tried to hide it.

"Harry, what's going on right now?" I pressed. "What's happening?"

"I'm apologizing."

"For?"

"Everything. From the very beginning, Simone, from the first moment we met, I knew that you were different. And I knew that I wanted to get to know everything I could about you," he started. "And once I got to know you, it didn't take me long to fall in love with you. How could I not fall for you? You're the best person I've ever met, Simone Didier. Anyone would fall in love with you."

"You're in love with me?" Everything went completely still around me. "Harry—"

"I hate what I did to us. I hate that I decided to turn that spark between us into an opportunity to lie to my family just so I could keep the magazine. I hate that I made you go along with it. I hate that I made it impossible for us to be anything real, because I kept pushing it all away. I hate that I pushed you away, too, Simone, because I can barely go five minutes without thinking about you."

Harry paused for a moment before he went on. "I don't think I know how to exist without you anymore, Simone. I don't know if I could ever go back to that."

"Harry—"

"I want us to be together, Simone. I want every moment between us to be real," he continued, his gaze focused on mine. "And I want to be there for our baby. I want us to be a family."

"Simone is pregnant?" Sean said from behind Harry. "Good job, big bro!"

"Sean! Shh! You're ruining the moment!" Ruby nudged him in the shoulder before she offered me an encouraging thumbs-up.

"Harry? Can we go somewhere more private?" I asked. "I think we really need to talk. Just us."

"Of course." Harry reached for my hand and began to lead the way. "Let's go somewhere where it's just us."

37

SIMONE

"Hi," I started with a whisper.

"Hi," Harry replied. He stood facing me.

We were standing in a small storeroom, the scent of coffee surrounding us on every side. Harry's family was still waiting for us out in the coffee shop's main lobby, which I knew because I could hear them chatting away, the sound of their voices filling the space between us.

"What is all this, Harry?" I pressed. "You invited me to your birthday party, but you're having it at the coffee shop? No way that's what you had in mind."

"Maybe I was just really craving a good cup of coffee."

"If you wanted a good cup of coffee, you could've had one imported from anywhere in the world. You didn't have to come here." I shook my head. "But you wanted both of us to be here. Why?"

"Because I love you, Simone. Because I wanted to get your attention. Because I wanted to apologize and I wanted you to believe that I meant it."

"Harry—"

"I'm sorry. I'm so, so sorry for being such an asshole to

you about the pregnancy. You never deserved that, especially from me—"

"So, what? All of a sudden you're okay with the idea of having a kid together?"

"I'm okay with the idea of having a kid with you. That's what I'm trying to say. I'm okay with the idea of doing anything with you, Simone, as long as we're doing it together."

Harry closed the space between us, his face inches away from mine. "I just want to be with you, Simone. That's it. Just tell me what I need to do and I'll make it happen. As long as I get to be with you."

"And you don't think I'm a gold digger?"

"Not at all. That was just me being a fucking idiot. I was terrified of everything, so I was just... making up monsters. Like a kid making up monsters under the bed." He laughed at his own response. "Shit. That sounded so much better in my head."

"Yep. Sort of sounded like you were calling me a monster." I laughed now, too. "Not the greatest thing to say when you're going for an apology, to be honest."

"Want me to try again?"

"Nope. I prefer the real thing." I beamed back at him. "And I love you, too, by the way."

Harry let out a sigh of relief. "Thank God. All of this would've been so awkward if you didn't—"

I interrupted what he was saying with an eager kiss, finally closing the distance between us. He returned the kiss with just as much excitement, his tongue soon slipping between my lips. We reached for each other then, my arms wrapping around him and his arms wrapping around me.

"Fuck, baby. I missed you. I missed you so fucking

much," he murmured as his mouth moved down toward my neck. "I love you so much, Simone."

He moved down toward the ground, his knees soon resting against the floor.

"Harry, wait!" Fear flooded through me at the thought of him going down on me with our families in the next room. "Don't—"

"Simone Didier, will you marry me? For real this time."

"Oh. Oh my God!" I now saw the diamond ring glistening inside of the ring box that Harry had just pulled out of his pocket. "Yes! Of course, I'll marry you! A million times yes!"

Harry grinned as he stood back up. He slid the ring onto my finger, then kissed me again.

"Did you really think I was going to go down on you? With everyone waiting for us out there?"

"No," I lied, before quickly admitting the truth. "Yes."

"Yeah. That's what I thought." Harry laughed. "Does this mean I can move back home? Now with the whole getting engaged thing?"

"Duh." I smirked. "If you didn't move back home, I'd move your stuff back in myself."

"Did he already apologize? Did Simone take him back?" I suddenly heard Taylor's voice from the other room. "Shit! I can't believe I got caught in traffic!"

"Want to go show off your ring?" Harry asked as he sweetly took me by the hand. "It sounds like people are getting restless."

"I think we should." I happily followed behind him as we made our way back into the coffee shop's main lobby.

As we made our way into the world for the first time as something real.

"Harry..." I bit my bottom lip as Harry lowered his head between my thighs. My dress was hiked up to my knees, and I was sitting on the edge of Harry's bed back at our house. It'd only been a few minutes since we'd made it through the front door, but it seemed like Harry just couldn't wait.

"Harry!" I groaned out his name as he dragged his tongue across my still-clothed clit, his mouth against my panties. He placed his hands on either side of my thighs, keeping my legs spread for him as he continued to tease me through the fabric. I whimpered, slightly embarrassed at how wet I was getting for him, even though he hadn't even touched my bare skin just yet.

But I couldn't help it. I wanted him just as much as he wanted me.

"Harry, please," I begged. "Please touch me."

Harry moved his mouth away from me, and his hands went up toward my panties. A few seconds later, he was pulling them off, letting them land on the bedroom floor. He then went right back to eating me, his tongue diving into my flesh before he brought it back up to my clit. I felt my thighs starting to shake, my body already thrumming with excitement.

"Harry," I whimpered again. "I'm coming, I'm coming..."

He moved his mouth even faster against me, even as I fell apart underneath him in the very best way. Before I knew it, Harry was moving me, his arms wrapped around me as he brought me toward the balcony of his bedroom. Once we were outside, he pressed my back against the nearest wall, giving me a perfect view of the night sky and the beautiful stars that decorated it.

He lifted me up, and my legs soon wrapped around his waist.

"Fuck!" I groaned as I felt his bare cock slide right into me. He wasted no time moving inside of me, his shaft thrusting long and deep as I pressed my hands against his back for balance.

"Mine," Harry groaned as he continued to fuck me with everything he had. "You're all mine, Simone."

"I was always all yours," I admitted, my pussy tightening around his cock. "Always."

He moved his head toward mine and kissed me, his shaft still pushing me closer and closer to the edge. I kissed him back, just as a moan ripped through me, my body already coming for him all over again.

He finished a few moments later, filling me up with his cum. I pressed small kisses all along his forehead as his movements slowed against me, his breaths coming shallow and quick.

We stayed like that for a bit, with the night breeze blowing across our skin, with him inside of me and my legs wrapped around him. It was a closeness that I'd never felt with anyone else before, one that went beyond physical compatibility or anything else I could've tried and failed to measure it by.

It felt like we were *one*. Harry and me.

Like we were just sharing the same soul in two different bodies.

38

SIMONE

Six Months Later

"I still can't believe how much you love these pretzels." Harry laughed as he handed me a huge bag of sour cream and onion pretzels. "But if it makes you happy, I'll keep buying them until they run out at the store."

I happily accepted the pretzels as I lay in bed. Dr. Carlson had put me on partial bed rest a few months ago, but now, I was expected to be in bed pretty much full-time. It was scary at first, depending on other people to handle everything for me.

But Harry had proven himself to be a fantastic caretaker. He was watching over me throughout the whole pregnancy, even taking a leave of absence at work to make sure he could help me himself.

"Thanks for the pretzels." I sighed before opening the bag. "Sometimes, these are the only things I can keep down."

I was still suffering from pregnancy-related nausea. It'd

shifted from morning sickness into general bloat among other issues, but Dr. Carlson assured me it was all perfectly normal. Thankfully, everything else was going well so far.

"I know, baby." Harry sighed, too, as he gently ran a hand across my abdomen. "Our little guy is giving his mom hell, isn't he?"

I smiled as soon as he'd said it.

Our little guy.

That'd become Harry's favorite nickname for our baby. We hadn't figured out a name just yet and had been trying out different nicknames in the meantime. I'd just been saying 'the baby,' but Harry had never been on board, claiming that our son needed to be called something more special than that.

Of course, that just turned into yet another reason to love him, seeing the way he already loved our son. Seeing the way he demanded better things for a kid who wasn't even here yet.

"How's Sean doing?" I asked before biting into another pretzel. "Has he run *LA Now* completely into the ground? Or is the building still standing?"

"Oh, he's trying his best to run it into the ground, definitely." Harry chuckled. "But I'm still helping him steer the ship. He's actually doing a lot better than I expected."

"Hmm. Maybe you never had anything to worry about? If he took over the company?"

"Ha! No." Harry shook his head. "Sean couldn't do this by himself. But maybe I could think about him working with the company someday, if he really wanted to."

"I'm happy you two are getting so close."

"Yeah, well, he pretty much saved our wedding. Hard to not get close to him after that."

I laughed a little at the memory. After we got engaged,

Harry and I decided to do everything over again, including our wedding and honeymoon. This time around, we'd chosen to get married on the beach, right at sunset, so we'd be able to capture the beauty of it in all of our wedding photos.

The only problem? The photographer was running late. She was running so late that we almost missed our preapproved wedding window, which would've meant either getting married in the dark or having to schedule it on a different day altogether.

But that's where Sean saved the day. It turned out that one of his best friends was a talented photographer. A photographer who happened to be attending the wedding.

It was obvious when we saw the photos after the wedding, each one expertly framed. Sean also took over the photography for the reception, too, choosing to snap photos of the party instead of drinking and dancing the night away. It was the sort of selflessness that Harry had never seen from his brother before, and it'd seemed to stay with him. Ever since then, Harry and Sean had grown so much closer.

Then again, Harry had seemed to grow closer with all of his family over the past few months. I couldn't put into words how glad it made me to see all of them coming together, with Harry finally finding his place among them.

"I think I need to go to the bathroom." I frowned as I started to shift out of bed.

But before I had a chance to even put my feet on the floor, I felt Harry reaching for my waist.

"Harry? What are you doing?"

"You said you needed to go to the bathroom."

"Right."

"I was just going to carry you so it's easier," he replied.

"That way, you don't have to put too much strain on yourself."

"It's not putting too much strain on myself to walk to the bathroom." I lightly chuckled. "I think you're being a little paranoid right now."

"Just let me?" Harry grinned, like he knew he was overreacting, too. "Come on. It'll be fun for both of us."

"Fun?"

"Interesting. Stress-free. Whichever word you think works best," he said as he reached for me again. I leaned into him as he started to pick me up.

But almost as soon as he did, I felt something wet running down my leg.

"Put me down! Put me down!" I pressed against Harry's chest until he set me back down on my feet.

"Simone? Baby? Are you okay?"

"Uh, I think my water just broke?" I stared down at the floor. "I think I'm—I think we're about to have a baby?"

I didn't know why every sentence was coming out like a question, but I couldn't stop myself.

"Holy shit! Holy shit!" Harry panicked before he reached for his phone. "We've got to get you to the hospital. I'm calling the car right now!"

∼

The drive to the hospital was a complete blur.

The only thing I was able to focus on were the contractions, the pain shooting through my body each time one rolled through me. I'd had a few contractions before, but nothing like this.

Nothing that felt like it was going to rip me apart.

The next thing I knew, I was being rolled into a hospital

room. I could tell that my surroundings were nice, the room seeming to be extra spacious. There were even flowers in the windows, but I didn't know if those were always there or if Harry had somehow arranged for those beforehand.

"Simone? How are you doing?" Harry asked, his face suddenly appearing in front of mine.

"I'm having a baby."

"Yes, sweetheart. You are." Harry smiled before he kissed my forehead. "You're having our little guy."

"Can I have the epidural now?"

"Yeah. Yes. Of course. I'll go and find the doctor." Harry smiled again, even though he seemed flustered. "Shit. I think I forgot the go-bag."

"That's okay. You can always go back and get it. Or have someone else pick it up and bring it over."

"Right, right." Harry let out a shaky breath. "We can deal with that later."

"One thing at a time."

"One thing at a time." He nodded. "I'll go get your doctor first. And then the rest."

Harry disappeared, and I closed my eyes, trying to focus on something other than the contraction pain.

It was interesting seeing Harry rattled like that.

It was a pretty rare look for him, since he always seemed to be in control of every situation, even when he wasn't. Even during our wedding photography disaster, Harry had kept calm, trying his best to come up with a plan on his feet.

But right now?

Right now, his nerves were so shot that if someone bumped into him, he might've imploded on the spot.

I smiled to myself, amused at the idea of an oh-so-rattled Harry O'Donnell.

A few moments later, he returned to the room with the

doctor in tow. She offered me a bright smile just as a second doctor walked into the room behind them. I watched as the doctors spoke to each other, and before I knew it, they were helping me roll over on the bed. The anesthesiologist delivered the epidural, and I took long, slow breaths.

And soon, everything melted into blissful numbness.

I couldn't feel much of anything anymore, at least not physically. Emotionally, though, I was struggling to keep it together. Without the physical pain to focus on, the only thing I had to think about were the million things that could go wrong at any point during the delivery.

Harry was right beside me the whole time, holding my hand. I gripped his hand in return, probably too tightly, as fear flooded my system.

What if something went wrong? What if I wasn't strong enough for this?

Harry kept his attention on me, his calm demeanor having returned. With every push, I looked to him for support, taking heart when there wasn't any worry or concern on his face. It was hard for me to keep track of what the doctor and nurses were saying, but I didn't have to.

Because all I needed to do was look at Harry, and I knew everything was going to be just fine.

~

"There you are. There's my little guy," Harry cooed as he rocked our baby back and forth.

I watched them through sleepy eyes, my body now feeling extremely tired after the delivery. The doctor had offered me the chance to hold the baby first, but I was so tired I could barely move my arms. I was afraid I'd drop the baby, so I was happy enough to watch Harry hold him for now, anyway.

"Lucas, are you being good for your daddy?" I asked, half-asleep.

"Lucas?" Harry asked, then paused for a moment.

And then his eyes creased with a wide smile. "Lucas. That's the perfect name for him."

"I can hold him now." I felt my strength returning, and I reached for the little bundle. Harry carefully handed him over, and I brought him up to my chest.

I stared into my son's blue eyes, moving my hand over his perfect face.

I was officially in love.

"Hi, baby. You're perfect." I smiled down at him, right on the verge of breaking into tears. "And you smell so good. That new baby smell is a real thing, huh?"

"Did you always want to name our baby after your dad?" Harry smiled as he asked. "Because you could've just told me. I would've been happy to name our son after him."

"After my dad?" It took me a few seconds to piece everything together. "Oh my God. I think I just accidentally named our son after my dad. I wasn't even thinking. It just came out—"

"I love it," Harry cut me off as he reached for my hand. "I think it's perfect, Simone."

"Good." I let out a tired sigh. "I hope Lucas likes his name, too."

I felt my eyes closing, my mind drifting off to another planet. By the time I opened them again, I was surrounded by our family, everyone gathering in the large room. Out of the corner of my eye, I spotted my mom, slowly making her way through the door using her walker. Harry's dad was holding the door open for her.

"Can I hold him?" Grace asked as she looked over at Harry. Harry handed his mom our son, and she softly squealed as she took hold of him. "Oh, little Lucas. I can't wait until you're older. We're going to have so much fun playing in the backyard together."

"Lucas?" My mom's voice was low as she walked over to Grace. "His name is Lucas?" Mom smiled at me, her eyes welling with tears. "Thank you, Simone. Your father would've loved that his grandson was named after him."

"Hold on. When's it going to be my turn to have a look at him?" Harry's dad joined the conversation. "Why do men always get to hold the baby last?"

"Oh, hush." Grace laughed. "Lucas, that's your granddad. And no, he's absolutely never going to change."

Jonah laughed now, too, as he stared down at the baby.

"He's so little," Maxon said, in awe at the baby. "Look at his tiny fingers!"

Ruby laughed. "You were that little not so long ago."

Maxon's eyes widened. "I was."

I laughed, then my attention drifted back to Harry, who smiled at me.

He moved closer to me, so close that he was able to whisper, "This is the happiest day of my life."

"Mine too," I whispered as my heart warmed in my chest. "I love you so much, Harry."

"I love you so much, too." He squeezed my hand and brushed the hair off my forehead. I settled against the pillows, once again letting myself drift off to sleep, knowing that everything was going to be okay.

Because I had Harry. Because I had my son.

And because we were one big, happy family.

EPILOGUE

HARRY

Four Years Later

"Dog! I want to get a dog!" Lucas greeted me with the request as soon as I stepped through the door. "Mommy said I have to ask you first."

I'd just gotten home from work, but it was only 5:00 p.m., so it was still pretty early. Gone were the days when I'd spend half the night working in my office, getting home so late it was almost time to go right back to work again.

Because now, there were more important things in my life than just work.

"Is that what Mommy said?" I hummed, pretending to think the question over. Simone and I had already agreed that we should get a dog for Lucas; it was just a matter of him picking one out. "Well, I think..."

"Yeah? Yeah?" Lucas's face lit up with excitement. "What do you think?"

"I think that it sounds like a good idea to me." I smiled down at him. "Let's get a dog."

"Yay!" Lucas broke into a cheer before he ran across the house. "Mommy! Daddy said yes!"

"How exciting!" Simone said as she walked into the living room, playfully shaking her head. "If he's this hyped up about just the idea of getting a dog, how's he going to be when he actually gets one?"

"Oh, he's going to lose his mind." I walked over to Simone before wrapping her up in my arms and pressing a kiss against her lips. "And how was your day, baby?"

"Um, I've got some news."

"News?" I pressed. "Good news? Bad news?"

"I think I might be pregnant again."

"You're not sure?" I frowned. "You haven't been to see Dr. Carlson yet?"

"Why do you sound a little disappointed?" Simone tilted her head to the side. "Wait. Are you actually excited about this? Do you actually *want* me to be pregnant?"

"More than anything," I admitted with a laugh. "I love being Lucas's dad. And I don't think I'd mind having a few more running around."

"A few more?" Simone rapidly blinked. "Harry, how many kids are you talking about?"

"That depends. How many do you think we have room for?"

"Two." Simone laughed. "I think two's a good number to stop at. It's a good, round number."

"Then two it is." I kissed her again. "But you should really go see Dr. Carlson. Just to be sure everything's on the right track."

"I will—"

"Mommy! Daddy! Can we go get a dog now?" Lucas ran back into the room.

"Not right now, sweetie," Simone answered before she

scooped him up into her arms. "But we can go look at photos of dogs online. We can see if there are any you like at the local shelter. And then, after you pick one out, we can go see if it's still there tomorrow."

"Okay, Mommy." Lucas sweetly kissed her on the cheek. "Thank you!"

"What do you think? Beef or chicken?"

The golden retriever puppy cocked his head sideways as he stared up at me. He'd been living with us for a few weeks now, and even though he was Lucas's dog, he was definitely Simone's and my responsibility.

"Does that look mean beef? Because I think it does." I finished setting out some wet dog food for him on the kitchen floor. "But if you don't like it, just let me know and we can get you something else."

"Are you talking to the dog again?" Simone laughed as she came into the kitchen. "You two are always having your own little private conversations."

"I don't know what to tell you, baby. The dog just gets me." I grinned before I went on. "How was your appointment with Dr. Carlson? Does everything look good?"

"Yeah. Everything looks fine." Simone seemed nervous. "Do you remember when we were talking about how many kids we wanted to have? And I said two, and you said—"

"However many we can fit in the house. Yeah."

"Right. That." Simone let out a shaky breath. "Well, it looks like you might've won out on that one."

"What do you mean by that, baby?"

"I mean that we're not going to have two kids," she

replied, her voice low. "Dr. Carlson let me know that we're actually going to have three."

"Three?" My eyes went wide. "Wait. Simone, are we going to have *twins*?"

Before she had a chance to answer me, I pulled her in close, keeping her tight against my chest.

She laughed. "Yes. We're having twins."

"I can't believe it. Twins!"

"But then, that's it, right?" Simone pleaded. "Because I'm pretty sure three kids would make a full house."

"We could always add more rooms. Or turn a few guest rooms into permanent bedrooms."

"I cannot believe you right now." Simone laughed again. "What happened to the guy who didn't even want *one* kid?"

"He realized that you, Lucas, and any babies we have in the future are the best things that could've ever happened to him."

"You're the best thing that happened to me, too, Harry." Simone sighed happily. "I'm so happy we found each other."

She buried her face against my chest as I squeezed her tight. For a moment, I thought about how easily this could've gone wrong, how close we'd come to calling the whole thing off and never speaking to each other ever again years ago.

How close we came to making the biggest mistake of our lives.

But that wasn't what happened. And because of my family's ridiculous tradition, because I'd cut in front of a girl in line at the coffee shop, because I'd been brave enough to admit when I was wrong and fight for what we had instead of letting it slip through my fingers...

I ended up with more than I ever could've asked for.

"I love you," I said to Simone, lifting her chin so I could gaze in her eyes.

"I love you, too."

It was the perfect moment.

It was more than I'd ever dreamed of.

Best of all, things would only get better from here.

∼

Want more spicy boss romance?
Read Boss's Secret Baby!

When Carter sees my son for the first time...
Feels a fatherly connection that he can't describe,
He knows something is wrong.

I have a secret that's four years old.
And that secret needs a daddy.

Keep reading for your Sneak Peek!

SNEAK PEEK OF BOSS'S SECRET BABY!

About the Book

My new boss is my baby's daddy...
He just doesn't know it yet.

But when he sees my son for the first time...
Feels a fatherly connection that he can't describe,
He knows something is wrong.

Five years ago, Carter and I had one unforgettable night hours before he left town.
I tried to find him, but fate had other plans.

Now, five years later, he's back in town.
And my baby's daddy is my prick of a new boss.

The moment his intense soul piercing blue eyes lock on mine,
I know I'm in trouble.

I have a secret that's four years old.
And that secret needs a daddy.

Hopefully Carter needs a mama...

Can our second chance survive a secret this big?

Chapter 1: Isabelle

Five Years Ago

"Are you kidding me?" I cried out, staring at Ryan.

He sat back in his chair, nonchalant as hell, looking like he hadn't just ripped my whole world apart.

"Come on, babe. It's better this way."

I shook my head. I couldn't wrap my mind around the fact that Ryan had taken me out on a date night just to break up with me. Who arranges a break-up date?

"How is it better?" I asked, trying not to let my voice tremble or to sound like I was going to cry. Which was exactly what I felt like doing. "We've been together for two years, and you're just throwing it all away."

"I'm not throwing it all away, babe." He leaned forward, reaching for my hand over the table.

"Don't call me that," I said, snatching my hand away before he could touch me. "You're dumping me. You can go right back to using my name."

"Fine, Isabelle," Ryan said, making my name sound like it tasted bad in his mouth. "I'm trying to be nice here, but you're not being very open to me right now."

I barked a sarcastic laugh. "You're right, how thoughtless

of me. I'll take notes so next time you dump me, I'm more gracious about it."

He sighed. "Don't be like this."

I crossed my arms over my chest. "I'll be however the hell I want. You don't get to make demands anymore."

He shrugged. "Okay. Sure. I guess you're right."

Damn straight I was right. Ryan was dumping me. I suddenly realized there was no reason I had to be here. He'd said his piece—we were over. He'd already explained that he wasn't ready to make a commitment. There was nothing left for me to do or say here.

I stood to leave.

"Wait," Ryan said. "We're not going Dutch on the check?"

My mouth dropped. "Get the check yourself, asshole," I said and turned around, marching away from him.

I bit back my sobs until I was out of the bar where we'd met, and at least halfway down the road to the bus stop. When the tears finally rolled down my cheeks, a sob racked my throat.

I fished for my phone and called June.

"He dumped me," I sobbed into the phone.

"What? Izzy, oh, my God!"

"I know," I said. "He invited me out for drinks. We had a beer, and then we ate that greasy pub food I love so much. And then he dumped me. After we'd had a good afternoon together."

"I can't believe it," June said. "I have to get Bernie into this call, too."

I nodded, waiting for June to dial Bernadette into the call so we were on a three-way. My two best friends were saints, always there for me when shit hit the fan.

And shit had just hit the fan in a big way.

We were all in college together. After sharing a dorm room the first year, we'd been attached at the hip ever since.

"Izzy, are you okay?" Bernie asked when she hopped on the line. "June told me before connecting me."

"I'm fine," I lied. I felt like collapsing on the curb in a puddle of tears.

"He doesn't deserve you," Bernie said fiercely.

"I stuck him with the check this time. We usually split it," I said. For some reason, I felt bad about doing that. But that was my problem—I was too nice. I always ended up getting walked over because I was nice and I didn't want people to go out of their way for me. So, I ended up putting myself second.

All the time.

I was a secondary character in my own story when I should have been the main character who took all the glory.

And this just proved it. Not even Ryan wanted to be with me anymore.

"It's good you made him pay," June said. "I wish you could have stuck it to him more, really made his life hell somehow."

Bernie agreed.

"I don't want to make his life hell," I said. "I just... want to move on."

That wasn't going to be so easy. I was still fixated on Ryan. Hell, until half an hour ago, I hadn't even known anything was wrong between us. I was just starting my last year at college, and he finished last year. We'd been talking about moving in together, about seeing what the rest of our lives would hold. I'd been ready for the long haul with him.

And he hadn't been able to see past today.

I swallowed down a sob.

"Do you know what you need?" June asked. "A

rebound," she added before I could guess. "You need to get out there and get in bed with a hottie that will make you forget all about that idiot."

"Excellent idea! Don't waste any time on that loser," Bernie agreed enthusiastically.

"I don't know, you guys..." I wasn't really the type to sleep around. I was a long-term relationship gal through and through. One-night stands weren't my thing.

"We should go out," Bernie suggested. "We can drown your sorrows in alcohol. When you're too drunk to judge if the guy is hot enough to take home with you, we'll help you decide." She sounded triumphant.

"I'm working tonight," I said.

I reached the bus stop and came to a stop.

"Come on," June groaned. "Cancel your shift."

"I can't do that. Besides, I'm saving up money for..." I didn't know how to finish that sentence. I'd been saving up money so that Ryan and I could get a place after college. Now, that wasn't going to happen. But I would still need a place to stay, whether it was with him or not. My stomach turned. God, all of this was so unexpected. And so unfair.

The bus rumbled toward us.

"I have to go," I said. "I'm working my shift, and then I'm going to bed. We'll talk tomorrow."

The girls protested about not being able to take me out for a short while longer, but then they gave in, and I ended the call. I climbed onto the bus, feeling numb, and I sat in one of the seats close to the back. I leaned my head against the window and watched the city slide by as the bus snaked through the streets of Los Angeles, taking me back to my student housing.

My shift at Café Noir started at five, and it ran until one in the morning. The café was a simple place during the day, offering food and artisan coffee. At night, we whipped out the cocktail menus and craft beers, and the crowd shifted from sensible daytime workers to raucous students.

I liked working there—it always had a good vibe, and since I'd worked at the café almost as long as I'd been studying, it felt like a home away from home.

"Hey, Izzy," my coworker Jimmy said when I clocked in for my shift and he clocked out. "Are you okay? You look..."

"I'm okay," I said before he could finish his sentence. "Just a tough week with classes and tests."

"You have some days off coming up soon, right? Then you can rest," he said.

"Yeah, that's a good point," I agreed, and he gave me a sympathetic smile before he left.

I walked to the counter, ready to serve the customers coming in for the late afternoon rush, and tried not to think about Ryan.

It would be no use if I cried into someone's coffee. That was just unprofessional.

Time ticked on, and the drinks changed from coffee to cocktails when the dinner orders started coming in. I worked hard, running back and forth. My mind kept jumping to Ryan, and when I forced it away, I thought about what June and Bernie had suggested—a rebound. But I couldn't do that.

Could I?

I'd been in a two-year relationship until today. I'd been thinking long term. My mind had been on the future, not on the present, and not on getting my physical needs met. Instant gratification had been the last thing I'd wanted.

I felt like the rug had been ripped out from under me.

"Two black coffees, and the best stout you have on tap," a deep voice said. I looked up.

Oh. My. God.

The bluest eyes I'd ever seen pierced me, and they were set in a face that could only have been carved by the angels. He was the epitome of tall, dark, and handsome, with tanned skin that made him look like he went for morning runs on the beach, broad shoulders, a confident attitude, and a grin on his face that made my stomach flutter.

"Coming right up," I managed to say, which was a damn miracle because the sight of Mr. Hot-as-Hell had made me feel all tongue-tied. I turned away from him and started preparing his order. Two coffees and a stout—that was the order, right? Good thing he'd said it before I'd seen his face because I wouldn't have heard a word he said.

What was wrong with me? I didn't usually notice guys like this. But if they looked like him, I'm sure I would have looked twice. Relationship or not.

When I'd prepared the two coffees, I put them on the counter.

He smiled at me and my heart skipped a beat.

"Let me just get that beer," I said.

He nodded, and I walked to the beer taps to pour the stout. I took the pint glass to the counter and put it down, calculating the price in my mind.

He pulled out a handful of bills and smiled at me again.

Cue the butterflies.

"Keep the change," he said.

"Thanks. Here you go," I said, offering him a tray for the coffee and the beer so that he wouldn't have to juggle them all.

"Thanks," he said. He flashed me that grin and walked away.

The conversation had been simple. But I shivered, my

stomach tightening again, and I watched him walk to a table with another man and a woman.

My stomach sank a little. Was he taken?

I snuck glances at him the rest of the night while I worked, watching the body language of his group. They were too far away from the counter for me to hear what they were saying, and as the evening picked up and I got busier, I could focus on them less and less. But at some point, the other man leaned over and kissed the woman, and I was oddly satisfied.

They were a couple. Mr. Dreamy was a third wheel.

Which didn't by any means tell me he was single—a man that attractive had to have a woman who was supermodel material. But still, a girl could hope.

They stood and left, and my stomach sank again when the table was empty. I would have liked to at least talk to him again.

But men like him didn't happen to women like me.

Just as well. I didn't need to get hurt another time.

It would have been nice, though, if at least one thing in my life worked out the way it did in the movies. Since I'd already lost my happy ending and all, I was due for some sort of good luck.

I wiped down the counter and glanced at the clock. It was getting close to midnight and business was dying down. We were closing up soon.

Someone walked up to the counter and cleared his throat.

When I looked up, I froze. Once again, I was caught in the gaze of Mr. Blue Eyes.

Chapter 2: Carter

Fuck, she was cute. Not just cute, smoldering hot, too. But something about the way she looked at me, the way her mouth perpetually looked like it wanted to curl into a smile, made me want to talk to her.

"Hi, Isabelle," I said when she looked up at me, blinking like I was some kind of vision.

She glanced down at her name tag, which was where I'd found out her gorgeous name. Then she looked back up at me.

"Hi," she said. "Can I... can I get you something? I think our kitchen is closed." She was flustered, and that made her even more attractive.

And she was already a stunner, with red hair that hung over her shoulder in light curls, and big, round brown eyes that made me want to fall into them.

"Yeah," I said. "Your number."

She blinked at me. "What?"

"I'm a little forward," I said. "Sorry about that. You're just the most beautiful thing I've seen in a long, long time. And I can't pass up the opportunity to spend some time with you."

She blinked at me before her cheeks flushed.

"I'm not a thing," she bristled.

I laughed. Oh, God. Feisty, too. She was the whole package.

"I just told you you're beautiful, and all you heard was that I said thing?"

She shrugged. "I don't like being treated like the help."

I laughed again. "I wasn't trying to treat you like the help. Poor choice of words. You're the most beautiful woman I've seen in a long, long time. Is that better?"

She bit her lip, then nodded shyly.

Shit. Already, she was driving me wild. I smiled.

"And I do want to spend some time with you. Would you like to have a drink with me?"

She hesitated.

"There's still time before you close, right?" I asked.

"I'm not allowed to drink on the job," she said.

"Who's going to know?" I asked. "We're the only ones left."

When she looked around, she saw I was right. There weren't any other patrons left. Everyone had gone home for the night. It was five minutes to twelve, and there was still time for her to pour another couple of beers.

She turned it over in her mind, I could see her thinking. And it was hot as hell.

"Okay," she finally said.

I grinned at her. "Okay."

She disappeared and a moment later, she returned with two beers.

We walked to the table where I'd sat with my college pal, Ray, and his girlfriend, Sonya.

"So, Isabelle," I said when we sat down.

"Most people call me Izzy," she said. "The name tag is formal." She touched her fingers to the tag on her chest.

"Izzy." Sassy. I liked it. "I'm Carter."

She smiled. "Hi, Carter."

I smiled at the sound of my name on her lips.

"So, Izzy, what do you do? Besides work here?"

"I'm a student," she said. "Art major."

I whistled through my teeth. "That's impressive."

"Is it?"

"For sure," I said. She looked shy under the compliment.

I had a lot of respect for art students. It was a difficult career path—it was all about passion to them because most of them didn't make it far in the art world. Making money from something like that, no matter how passionate you were about it, was hard.

"What about you?" she asked.

"I finished college last year. I'm just wrapping up an internship now."

"So, what's next for you, then?" she asked.

I took a swig of beer. "Business school."

"Really?"

I nodded. "I want to make a difference, you know? But not in the way most people say they want to."

"How, then?"

"Gourmet food."

She laughed, and I was in trouble. I could get addicted to that sound.

"Hey," I said, poking her lightly in the shoulder and loving the contact. "Good food brings people together. And it makes a profitable business, too."

"I like your enthusiasm. Where's your school?" she asked.

"New York."

Was it my imagination, or did her face fall?

I was flying out to New York City in two days to start graduate school. I'd worked hard to get where I was now, and I'd work even harder when I got to the Big Apple.

"When are you leaving?" she asked.

I hesitated, unsure if I should tell her. I didn't want to scare her off.

"In two days."

Her eyes widened. "Oh, that's soon."

I nodded.

Leaving was bittersweet. I loved LA, but I needed to take

this next step. An MBA would open a lot of doors for me. And I had big plans.

"Well, I'm sure you'll do well in grad school," Izzy said. "It sounds like you're passionate about your future business."

I nodded. "Absolutely. What's the point if there's no passion?"

"Exactly," she said. "That's why I'm studying art, even though I know what most people say about it."

"I think it's noble," I said. "What kind of art do you make?"

"I'm a painter," she said, her eyes lighting up.

"Ah. What do you like to paint?"

"Anything," she said, playing with a lock of her fire-red hair. "Landscapes, abstract. But portraits are my favorite. I love people's faces. They always tell a story."

She smiled at me. Her eyes were mesmerizing. I knew I was leaving soon, but I wanted to get to know her better. Something about her made me want to get closer, to find out what made her tick.

"Are you single?" I asked.

My question surprised me as much as it surprised her.

"Yeah," she said, and an expression flickered across her face too fast for me to read.

"Lucky me," I said and grinned at her.

She laughed, and it was beautiful. Rich and full and genuine.

"Yeah, I guess you are."

I took a sip of my beer. "So, what are you doing when you're not working at Café Noir or painting pictures?"

"Being a full-time student and working take up most of my time," she admitted.

"What are you doing tonight?" I asked.

She shrugged. "After locking up and erasing all signs of my breaking the rules right now—" she winked at me "—I'm probably going home to sleep. I have classes early tomorrow."

"That's too bad," I said.

"Why?"

"Because I was hoping you would come out with me to celebrate."

She blinked at me. "What are we celebrating?"

"The fact that I met the most beautiful woman I've ever seen." I grinned at her and watched as she blushed bright red.

"Oh, you are smooth, Carter. But meeting me is hardly cause for celebration."

"Oh, Isabelle," I said, leaning forward. "Have you seen you?"

She blushed again and I reached forward, touching her arm. I couldn't help myself. She was magnetic.

"So, what do you say?" I asked. "When you're done here, do you want to come with me?"

"Where are we going?" she asked in a breathy voice.

"Wherever you want."

"For someone who looks so put together, I'd think you'd have an answer ready for that question," she said.

I laughed. "You think I look put together?"

"Don't you?" she asked. "I mean, look at you." She slid her eyes over my body, and I relished the way she looked at me. "You're definitely the type of guy to command a boardroom."

I laughed. "Is it that obvious that I'm a business major? I couldn't pass for a carpenter, or a lumberjack?"

She raised her eyebrows. "Seriously? A lumberjack? I can just picture you in flannels and boots, sizing up a tree, wondering how much you'll have to bribe it to fall over for you."

I burst out laughing. "Bribe it?"

"Well, I can tell you work out," she said. "But you don't have the calloused hands of someone who runs a chainsaw for a living." She reached for me and took my hand in both of hers. At the contact, electricity jumped between us and my breath caught in my throat. She glanced up at me before studying my hand.

I loved the feel of her hands on mine, her skin soft and smooth, and her fingers able. She had paint spots on her hands, and the splotches were endearing.

I leaned forward so that our heads were bowed together, studying my hand.

"So, you think I'll be better at closing deals than chopping down trees?" I asked. My voice was a little hoarse.

She glanced up at me again and her face was so close to mine, I could see the flecks of gold dancing in those big brown eyes.

"Yeah. And it's better for the environment."

I chuckled. I could smell her shampoo. I lifted my free hand and tucked her hair behind her ear. Her eyes were locked on mine, and when I leaned in to kiss her, she closed her eyes.

When our lips touched, it was the same incredible electrical surge that pulsed through me as when she'd touched my hand. I slid my tongue into her mouth and she moaned softly.

The sound was erotic, and it made my cock stiffen in my pants.

I cupped her cheek and kissed her more urgently, trying to show her the effect she was having on me. I moved my hands to her back, sliding them over her shoulders and up to her hair as I pulled her closer. Her arms wrapped around my shoulders. I inhaled her scent, intoxicated.

When we finally broke apart to look at each other, she was out of breath as if she'd run a mile, and her eyes were darker, deeper. Her lips were slightly parted.

"Come home with me," I said.

She leaned back a little.

Shit, did I blow it?

"I have to clean up and lock up the café," she said.

I nodded. "I'll help you."

We stood together. All the other employees had gone home, and I helped her close up. We tipped the chairs onto the tables for the cleaning crew to come in the morning, wiped the counters down, and she switched on the large industrial dishwasher that someone had loaded earlier.

The whole time, I couldn't stop staring at her. I watched her as she moved, keeping track of her as we worked. She was elegant and graceful, doing everything with care, as if it really mattered. Her long red hair was like a flame as she moved beneath the dim lights. When she glanced at me now and again, her eyes were deep. Her expression suggested she was as eager to get out of here as I was.

When the shop was ready, and she'd locked the door, she turned to me.

"I don't usually do this," she announced.

"What? Have help cleaning up the shop?"

She giggled. "No. Go home with someone I just met. It's not usually... my style."

"Okay," I said. What if she changed her mind? I desperately needed her, but I didn't want to persuade her to do something she didn't want. "Are you sure you want to do this?"

"Yes, I am. But I just wanted you to know that."

I nodded. "Noted. And I'm honored."

She nodded, too.

"So, which way?" she asked.

I took her hand and lifted it to my mouth, brushing my lips against her knuckles.

"This way," I breathed and led her to my car.

Chapter 3: Isabelle

I was going home with him.

I hardly recognized myself. A one-night stand? And what was more, I was fresh out of a relationship. That was who I was— the long-term relationship girl.

And where had that gotten me?

Dumped, and feeling like crap because Ryan didn't think I was good enough to commit to.

And that was totally bullshit.

Maybe I wasn't like some of the other girls who ran around campus, who had a ton of friends and big trust funds, but I had some good things going for me.

And Carter could see that. He talked to me like I was worth something.

I realized that for a long time, Ryan had made me feel small. I had been so caught up in our dream of 'forever' that I hadn't noticed how he'd started disregarding me, and how he'd started treating me like I was a maybe in his life, when he'd been a definitely in mine all that time.

Carter looked at me like I was the only woman in the world. Even though it was just for tonight, the way he treated me felt good.

We rode with the windows down. He moved his hand to my leg and interlinked his fingers with mine. It was sexy, but sweet, too. Everything about him, every little move he made, was perfect.

His car was nice. Expensive, but not in a flashy way. I liked that about him—he was obviously higher on the economic food chain, and he had a few doors already open for him in life. But he didn't give me the idea that it defined him. He didn't rub it in my face or make me think he was just using it to get me in bed.

And that made me want to get in bed with him all the more.

Still, Carter was a stranger. And I didn't go home with strangers. I'd always had a theory that going home with strangers was asking for trouble. But when I thought about Ryan, I realized that even though I'd thought I knew him all this time, it turned out that I really hadn't known him all that well. I would have never thought he would throw away something we'd worked on for so long...

For no reason at all.

And Carter... there was something about him that made him feel like he wasn't a stranger at all. When we talked, it was like he understood me. And I hadn't had that with anyone.

Not with Ryan, and not with any of the guys I'd dated before.

Not even with my girlfriends, to be honest. Not like this. I'd always figured it was because I was an artist. A little different from everyone else. I hadn't expected anyone to truly understand me.

But somehow, it felt like Carter did.

And that wasn't something I wanted to let slip through my fingers.

So when he'd asked me if I wanted to go home with him, the only answer that had made logical sense was 'yes.'

We arrived at his apartment and he unlocked the door, letting me walk in first.

"Oh," I said when he flicked on the lights and I looked around. "This place doesn't look anything like my student apartment."

My place was a little dingy, with water damage on the ceiling, an oven I had to wedge shut with a broomstick, and a door I had to put my body weight behind to open or shut if I wanted to come or go.

Carter's place was neatly outfitted with modern designer furniture, and it had a clean, masculine scent.

Carter chuckled when I ogled the place.

"It's not much, but it's home."

"Are you kidding me?" I asked. "If this is your definition of 'not much,' I don't want to know what the rest of your life will look like when you're some crazy business mogul."

I shrugged out of my coat and Carter took it for me. A real gentleman.

He laughed. "You think I'm going to become a business mogul?"

"Oh, yes," I said.

He certainly looked the part. I was pretty sure he would be drop-dead gorgeous in a designer suit.

He was already jump-his-bones hot.

All he needed was to take that commanding air a step further and he was going to be everything.

He cupped my cheek, his face close to mine.

"You're staring," he mumbled, his lips so close to mine I could barely concentrate on the words he was speaking.

"You're distracting," I said.

I sounded like a fool. But he chuckled, and his voice was thick and smooth and it caressed my skin like honey.

When he kissed me, it was just as electric as it had been

at the café when he'd pressed his lips against mine. But this time, it was different. There was so much more passion behind it. So much more lust. He pressed the length of his body against mine, and I could feel the bulge in his pants, proof of his growing interest in me.

And God, I wanted him. He was charming and handsome and confident—exactly the type of guy I never expected to end up with. And what was more, he wanted me, too.

I could feel it all the way down in his boxers, where his cock strained against his pants to get to me.

It was setting my body on fire, the way he ground himself against me. My stomach tightened. I was getting wet for him.

God, so wet.

Carter broke the kiss and looked at me.

"Can I get you something to drink?" he asked.

Was he serious? I didn't want anything to drink. Or to eat. Or anything that wasn't him naked and on top of me.

I blushed at myself, thinking things like this about a total stranger.

But then again, he didn't feel like a stranger to me.

I shook my head and kissed him, running my hands over his chest.

"I want to know where your bedroom is," I said.

Look for Boss's Secret Baby on Amazon!